THE SLOW COOKER

THE SLOW COOKER

by

SKENE. MacDONALD

HAMILTON & Co. Publishers
LONDON

Publisher

Hamilton & Co. Publishers
10 Stratton Street
Mayfair
LONDON

ISBN 1 901668 25 8

Acknowledgements

Sincere thanks and appreciation to the many friends who provided their support and helpful advice, including my wife and Mr J McCormack, McCormacks Printing Services, Cowdenbeath.

FOREWORD

It is probably not too well known that manure, in time, will decompose organic matter into jelly-like mass which will be extremely difficult to recognise.

CHAPTER ONE

It was during the month of May 1930, when events occurred to awaken the small Scottish village of Craigmire from that drowsy pre-summer state of inertia.

When the sun is mounting the sky to its zenith, the warm breeze bending the tall grass into shimmering waves of sunlight, and grain crops preparing to transform the landscape from the rich green to that golden promise of another harvest.

The countryside alive with the hum of the bee and the birds high in the sky filling the air with song.

The smell of clover, sweet and the fragrance of wild flowers in all their abundance.

1930: just ten years since the end of World War One and a nation reeling under the economic strain regarding some sanity in international communications and trade.

A time in history when those who had survived the slaughter found that the "Land fit for Heroes" was a myth as they formed tiresome queues at a Labour Exchange for a weekly hand-out and a fruitless quest for work.

Indeed, the Nation was recovering from the National Strike of 1926, when the "greedy' scored over the "needy'.

The result could be seen in the small groups of men gathered at the village well, where they spent time sharing yarns and waiting for the open doors of Joe Penman's pub, The Plough, when it would be possible for them to spend what little they had on their favourite brew.

Close by, surrounded by a spiked iron railing, the village school windows had been opened to relieve the stifling air in the classrooms.

Children's voices parroting the times tables, interrupted occasionally by a stern reprimand from the dreaded Mrs. Hawket.

The entrance to the school was marked in bold letters carved in stonework "Boys', "Girls'; segregating the sexes indoors and in the play area, where yet again, there was the evidence of the legacy of Victorian discipline in the form of spiked iron fence; a barrier, over which great penalties would be administered should any boy attempt to pass.

A policy, it may be observed, which reached the limits of the ridiculous when outwith the school boundary, boys and girls would make their way happily homewards, hand in hand.

Across the badly maintained Main Street, the bell above the entrance of the general store offered fair competition with the school bell which signalled the wild noisy stampede of youngsters celebrating their hard won freedom.

The general store included the local post office and a meeting place for all and sundry who savoured the mixed aroma of spice and flour bread and vegetables.

The local gossips dodged the oil lamps hanging from hooks on the ceiling, together with all kinds of implements from garden hoes to spades and shovels.

John and Lizzie Duncan were popular with the locals and skilled in their chosen role as interlocutor; avoiding personal commitment to any points of contention.

This was the pod which produced the seeds of scandal, where character was stripped and torn and whispered innuendo was exchanged from ear to ear and tongue to tongue.

Surprisingly, there seemed to be no evil intent behind the daily exchange of news, the latest "arrival in the village', "had she had a hard time?', "is it a braw bairn?'.

"Have ye heard aboot so and so? Well, she's goin' wi anither man'.

A typical Scottish village with its rows of pantile cottages, providing the bare necessities and for a few more fortunate than others the benefit of running water and electric light.

The village hall played an important part in the social life in the area. The Saturday night dance where boy met girl and many romances were begun amidst the noise of simple people enjoying an evening.

The concerts and the celebrations. It all happened in the village hall.

Sundays were noted for the procession of the "flock', following tradition as well as commitment in answer to the rather weak chime of the church bell.

The figures dressed in black, clutching their Bibles, were in their "Sunday Best'. That is to say, "The dress kept for special occasions - weddings, funerals and perhaps a trip to the town".

The manse, larger than the small church, with its seven rooms and a row of bells to summon a poorly maid servant to put another log on the fire, was surrounded by the customary high stone wall which served to provide the incumbent with that degree of privacy arrogantly accepted as a right by those who elevated themselves to a higher level on the social pyramid.

The Reverend Mathew Davidson, M.A carried out the duties he was called upon to perform. The weddings, the christenings and the funerals.

He served the community well, whilst other denominations were obliged to travel elsewhere in order to follow their chosen way.

When he emerged from the seclusion of the manse, the minister would acknowledge to touching of the forelock or the curtsey with a dignified inclination of the ordained head: his class-consciousness betrayed by the fact that he sent his two sons to a private boarding school in town.

As a matter of course, it was only natural that the lady of the manse, Mrs Davidson would be elected to the chair at all the various functions and meetings which took place in the village and in the Parish, but apart from these appearances, the minister's wife was rarely to be seen in the village.

Besides the school bell, the general store bell and the church bell, there was another sound which could be said to be in harmony with the life of the community. It was the noise of hammer on steel. That delightful tone identified as the anvil in the blacksmith's shop.

Sandy Thompson ran a busy "smithy', where three men skilled in the craft of the farrier kept the local horses well shod.

To many, it was a fascinating pastime to stand in the doorway, with the searing heat of the forges drifting past, watching the white hot metal taking shape under the hammer of the anvil. To see a strip of metal being formed into a horseshoe, strictly to size and to join others hanging on the walls. The "made to measure' stock-in-trade of the "Smith'.

Donald McKay was a farrier. He had served his time well under the watchful eye of the master craftsman, who usually acknowledged his approval with a nod and a grunt.

Another day's work done and he took of the leather apron and placed it on a hook on the wall.

Sandy Thompson too, was preparing to end a day's toil and soon the old man's apron was hanging alongside Donald's.

Sandy was five foot ten inches tall when he stood upright but now, with the passing of time and the nature of the heavy work he had performed over a period of many years, his broad shoulders were stooped and a huge carbuncle on his bald head, gave him an unquestionable identity. His bowed legs and his stoop, combined with a distinctive wobble from side to side was how Donald was always to remember this kind, old blacksmith.

The forges were damped down for the night and he set out for home where his mother would certainly be waiting with her famous pot of Scotch Broth, and a meal fit for a king.

Donald's father had died as a result of a tragic tree felling accident in the estate and his mother worked as a cleaner at the village school to provide for her son.

Together, they lived in the cottage, a "But-and-Ben'. Donald used the bedroom and his mother used the infamous boxed-in bed in the other room. This type of bed was merely a recess in the wall, fitted with wooden planks to support a mattress.

Donald had managed to build an extension to the rear of the house, which served as a kitchen and a suitable place in which a man could have a bath in a tin tub, supplied with hot water from the cast iron kettles kept on top of the coal-fired range.

Donald's tidy habits and immaculate turn-out in the Sunday best was due to much diligence on his mother's part. She had carefully nourished her boy and had taught him the value and merits of cleanliness and tidiness.

It was Saturday night and Donald's mind was far from the horseshoes and hot metals. He was in love. Thoughts of Monica, the farm manager' daughter were forever clouding his mind.

There would be a dance in the village hall tonight and he was on his way to the Home Farm, dressed as usual, in his "Sunday best'. His widowed mother saw to it that her Donald was always "well turned oot'.

His heart was on a "high'. It had always been that way with him, since his days at school. That was when the love affair begun.

She had been late that morning as she walked into the classroom, he saw her as if for the first time. Why hadn't he noticed this lovely girl before? Slim, and well proportioned, her dark fringe shading blue eyes.

His schoolwork became a casualty on that instant. The boy was in love, and the thrill of the experience disturbed all his emotions.

He wanted to be near her. He wanted to speak to her. He wanted to hear her voice. Above all else, he wanted courage. The courage to make the first attempt. To face that dreaded moment we all know so well, when the decision has been made and the commitment has arrived with no turning back.

The bond and the romance was initiated through the iron bars of that ridiculous iron fence which separated the boys from the girls.

Whenever the opportunity presented itself, he would take up a position near to where she would be standing.

At first, being near to her gave him a thrill, but that was not enough. He knew he must speak to her. He knew that he had first to pluck up enough courage to avoid that embarrassing collapse of vocal chords which can ruin the first few words, and their effect.

There she was, at the rails. Her back was to him. She was alone. This was his moment. He must talk to this girl.

"Monica", he heard himself say her name.

She turned to face him and smiled.

"You're Donald McKay', she said.

Her voice was music to his ears. "Aye, and I ken your name, Monica", he blurted out. Then boldly, "Can I see ye efter school?"

There, it was done. There was no turning back. "Of course, if ye want ti"

He couldn't believe it. She had actually accepted his boyish invitation to meet him.

Monica confessed later, that when their love affair matured, that she couldn't concentrate on her work that day. She kept on thinking about the boy with the broad smile and fair hair.

He had left the main road and his mind was reflecting on these bygone days, and the love which had changed the lives of the young blacksmith and the girl of his dreams.

There was no need to number the dwellings in the village. Each cottage was known by everyone living there. Known by the names of the occupants, the Brown's, and the Dufy's etc.

With so little recreational facilities to occupy their spare time, the villagers relied on traditional pastimes. The local concerts, the annual flower show, which usually stimulated great rivalry amongst the "experts' and in the rural setting the garden produce was essential towards survival.

In some of the gardens there would be a "Summerhouse', where the cronies would congregate and tell such wonderful tales of past glories, and, at times, questionable exploits which would be acknowledged by raised eyebrows and silent nodding unseen by the storyteller, revelling in a moment of self-imposed dignity.

It is often said "If only walls could speak', and there is no doubt that the village of Craigmire could offer a fair contribution to the social history of the land.

The pious, comprised the membership of the local church and consequently justified the so-called "Living' of the Parish minister.

The non-churchgoers, who could find their own spiritual inspiration in "The Plough' (Never let it be said).

A regular "bus service passed the narrow tar and chip road to the village which allowed weekly visits to the town, where the growing attraction of the cinema was insidiously "Americanising' the "Vernacular' exploiting the demand for relief from boredom, as well as an insight into new and perhaps questionable cultures where crime and violence was in increasing demand.

The images on the silver screens created the false impression of streets paved with gold and that the opposite sexes had very loose morals; sleeping with anyone available.

Donald and Monica had long since been recognised as two youngsters who were destined to marry and "settle-down', which generally meant that they would make their home in the vacinity of the village.

They were accepted as members, having been born in the village and had attended the village school.

Strangers, on the other hand, although they might be tolerated with caution, would forever be strangers.

Events which were soon to follow were set to change the lifestyle of this village without the numbers on the door.

CHAPTER TWO

The road leading to the Home Farm was a rough cart track, rutted and following the boundary of the fields.

The cloudless sky promised another pleasant evening. There was still warmth in the breeze, which swayed the crops and sighed through the trees.

Then suddenly, the first sign of the horror to come, was carried by that unseen movement of air. A heavy, disagreeable odour, which contrasted so vividly with the scents of nature.

It was overpowering. Donald was reminded of the previous encounters with the smell of dead animals.

The swarm of flies attracted his attention. It was inevitable that he would investigate the source of that pungent odour.

The flies swarming over the point at a ditch which passed around the edge of a field of corn created a sinister buzz. The air was alive and the sound indicated that the insects were extremely agitated.

Donald hated flies. He did not relish the idea of parting the ferns growing over the ditch, concealing whatever lay there.

Yet, it was necessary that he should satisfy himself that the unpleasant smell was indeed issuing from a dead animal.

He recoiled in shock. Lying face down in the trickling stream was the body of a young girl. Her hair was waving in the surge of water as it passed on over the rocks and through the weeds.

The lad retreated, swiping the flies who seemed to have chosen him for their next meal. He must report his find immediately.

It didn't occur to him to look elsewhere in the vacinity of the body in the ditch. Foremost in his mind was the urgency to report what he had seen.

His distress was obvious when he reached the farm. Monica knew immediately that there was something far wrong with her boyfriend. She did not hesitate, but she ran towards him and wrapped her arms around his neck.

This is how they both wished it to be. Close to each other. So close that only the fabric of her dress and his Sunday suit kept them apart. Their lips drank the sweet nectar of their mutual desire for the fulfilment of the ecstasy they shared.

David Anderson, Monica's father managed the Home Farm for the Laird. He employed six men and part-time employees as they were required.

During these post-war years the agricultural machinery had not reached the present-day mechanised efficiency, which has greatly reduced the demand for expensive labour.

The tractor was a clumsy alternative to horse drawn implements. The heavy iron wheels, with their spikes, lacked the advantage the subsequent introduction of pneumatic tyres provided.

Dave, as he was known, belonged to the "old school', who believed that the heavy monsters with their spiked wheels would impact the subsoil, restricting drainage and the spread of roots.

He was amazed at what Donald had to tell him about the body in the ditch, observing that the location indicated by the lad had not been visited for some time due to the development of the corn in the field.

They must report this matter to the police without delay.

Constable Hamilton, "Dick', to his friends, would puff the few miles he had to travel on the sturdy bicycle used by the rural policemen who were thinly spread around the area. It would take him at least half an hour to reach the farm.

Mrs. Anderson knew when to appear with her famous scones and her plum jam. There would be time to have a snack before Dick would make a breathless appearance.

The telephone system in use at that time depended upon the manual connection of lines and this was carried out in a local exchange, manned by ladies who were expert in selecting the right cable and placing it in the connecting socket.

Jennie Liddel was such an expert, and as well as her doubtless ability to make the right connection, she had another ability and that was to create a sensation. To elaborate and fantasise.

The indicator before Jennie flashed its signal.

"Exchange, can I help you?"

Jennie had the voice. She played the part efficiently.

"This is Dave Anderson at the Home Farm, can ye put me through ti the polis?"

Jennie was energised. The polis! Whit would Dave be wantin' wi' the polis?

"Ye're through", Jennie listened to every word.

The other girls seated in line at the consoles turned their heads towards the lady who had at last disturbed the otherwise monotonous drudgery of work on the exchange.

Dave Anderson was "phoning the polis!

This was news indeed. Jennie revelled in her moment in the spotlight. Her eyelids fluttered and her head shaking from side to side causing much impatience. The girls wanted to know what Jennie was listening to. They knew that they would have to wait.

The waiting was almost unbearable. They heard all kinds of odd affairs on the "phone and to give them their "fair due', they very seldom broke the code of silence which their particular duties demanded.

At last. At last. Jennie pulled the connection from its socket and, placing her hands on her knees, prepared to relish this moment when she could revel in the drama which she had shared with the polis and Dave Anderson.

"It's a body in the ditch". There now. Jennie savoured each moment as the girls gasped. "They've found a body in a ditch", Jennie repeated. Now this was indeed something to talk about. Such a change from the everyday topics, the latest film in town, the latest scandal, and all the other subjects enjoyed in the daily routine.

The switchboard was busier than usual after this initial news flash. Lizzie Duncan just had to be told and naturally, when Lizzie heard the exiting news, the entire community would be invited to share the sensation.

Little groups of residents were gathering, the women standing with their hands tucked under their breasts as was the custom, shaking their heads in disbelief. Speculating on who the victim would be, and could have carried out such a crime.

The village hall was lit. There was to be a dance that night, and the bandsmen were getting their instruments set up, ready for the reels and Strathspeys.

Saturday evenings brought people from many miles around to the hall and to the pub.

On this particular evening, the little Scottish settlement was the scene of great activity.

Joe Penman tapped another cask of beer. He was certain that news of the dead body would improve the takings of the till.

It was to be expected. Constable Hamilton was breathless when he arrived at the farm on his sturdy bike.

"Whit's this aboot a body?", he asked. "Can ye show me where it is?"

Donald told the constable how he had found the remains of a girl in the ditch.

"We'd better has a look then, Donald". Dave decided to accompany the constable and Donald to the scene of the crime. Somehow, he felt it his duty to give the lad all the support he could under the circumstances.

On their return to the farm, the constable "phoned his superiors in the town.

Busy Jennie Liddel heard it all, but on this occasion she didn't pass on what she had heard. She knew that the arrival of the police from the town would focus attention on her and the curious busybodies would pay a ransom for any snippet of information, which might add to the growing excitement. She had a "friend' in the local press offices, of course, and it was inevitable that Campbell would hear about the tragic discovery in the village. Campbell, a hard bitten reporter with "The Times'.

Five miles away, the tall chimneys on the horizon marked the location of the nearest town, where most of the local inhabitants found work in factories producing linen and other fabrics.

1930. Synthetic fibres had yet to be invented. Demand for natural yarns and threads ensured steady employment for the hordes of young women who make the daily trek to the "treadmills', where they toiled in conditions which would not be tolerated today.

As they entered the village, Inspector Reg Gilmour and Detective Constable Penman formed the vanguard of the investigating team.

The Inspector asked the way to the farm and was directed to the end of the main road through the village.

Murder wasn't and everyday occurrence and it would be some time before a team of experts could be organised.

The first consideration was to screen the area from prying eyes and this concerned the Inspector when he realised that the press had been alerted and were making their customary forceful way to the scene.

He told the D.C. to move forward to halt the advancing hoard of sensation seekers, knowing full well that he had given the man a very difficult task to perform.

The Press is forever a problem, carrying with it the justification for the aggressive methods used and that the public have a right to be told. "The public have a right to be told", they say in one voice and this raised the question about who may benefit from the broadcasting of intricate details related to whatever might be the subject of the matter and who could be implicated rightly or wrongly.

On so many occasions there are the precedents in the history of the press and its relationship with their so-called public, where justice has been the casualty, and the moguls behind the desks; the vultures who gleaned the profits.

There is so much that can be said for, or against the behaviour of the press, and in this particular instance it was obvious that information about the gruesome discovery in the ditch should not be released to the public.

Fortunately, reinforcements were soon to arrive, creating more dust on the farm road.

The murder team had brought all the necessary equipment to erect a canvas screen around the scene, and the investigation was underway.

Careful not to disturb any evidence which could have been left in the vicinity of the body, the team photographed every aspect, whilst others moved outwards in radius from the centre, examining closely every blade and stone.

Press cameras clicked and shadowy figures could be seen high in the branches of nearby trees, hoping, no doubt, to find a vantage point from which movements of the investigators might be observed.

The body was moved carefully into the wooden chest and the lid was lowered to ensure that every precaution would be taken to prevent any premature information leaking to the public.

During the operation, it was obvious that the swarm of flies had not abandoned their frenzied attack on the corpse. They buzzed around the box.

It was known that the insects would take every opportunity to deposit eggs on the dead flesh and in the natural course of events, to provide the resultant multitude of maggots - a feast to prosper where they were laid. The body was placed in the "Black Maria' police van and escorted on its way out of town.

Now was the time for questions.

The How? The What? The Why? and so on.

The identity of the victim would be a priority besides her age, condition and the all-important time of death.

Reg Gilmour was rather new to this kind of duty. Murder was not common in the rural district and he was conscious of the responsibility he acquired with the rank on his shoulders.

His quiet, unassuming demeanour concealed an unrelenting determination to seek out the facts which earned him the respect he was due from his subordinates.

The arrival on the scene by the Divisional Superintendent was obvious by the revival of the "Yes, sirs" and "No, sirs", which had somehow been neglected by the junior ranks in their exchanges with Reg and the Inspector.

Reg had long since learned the value of sharing the burden of decision-making with his subordinates. He allowed them freely to offer assistance and suggestions, and by doing so, earned their respect. Not quite the respect shown to the curt and abrasive senior rank, bearing all medals and arrogance his rank allowed.

The "Super" satisfied himself that all was well with the procedure taken so far and, climbing into his car, he sat back in the leather upholstery and gave the order to drive away.

CHAPTER THREE

Question time had arrived. It had to be door-to-door. Every possibility would have to be examined in detail.

The police had very little information to work on at this stage.

Had anyone been reported missing lately?

Who would use that farm road and when?

Had anyone seen any strangers in the area?

These country jobs were tiring. There was so mush distance between one cottage and another.

There is certain to be an eccentric person in a community. Someone who can be tolerated but generally treated with that degree of sympathetic interest that lacks credibility.

Aggie Wishart fitted the bill completely. The residents knew how she would fantasise and clamour for attention, and Aggie didn't let them down. It was said about her that "There wiz nae harm in Aggie but, Oh, how she bleathers".

Newspaper reporters were swarming as thickly as flies that day, each intent of finding that spark of interest which set alight the blaze of glory for the author of the prize "The Scoop".

Finding a body was something worth writing about. In fact, such a subject was rather unique in this neck of the woods. The incidence of crime was low - and murder? At this stage, with no positive details having been released by the police, any report by the media relied upon assumption and speculation.

Campbell, a seasoned and experienced man, with a pad and pencil spotted Aggie Wishart.

He had the "eye' for a good source of news, and all the cunning which goes with the struggle for survival when one faction is opposed to another.

Yes, Aggie would be a choice target for a news-hungry newsman.

"Hello, there". His approach was perfectly articulated to stimulate the ego.

Aggie was thrilled to be addressed by the man with the camera and the notepad.

She was already trimming loose hair from her forehead and, was that hand on the hip a tentative attempt at a posture for the pose she hoped she would be asked to make for the press?

Her name and her photograph in the newspapers! It all flashed across her simple mind when she was approached by this master at interrogation.

Campbell had the gift of taking the "thread' and weaving a web around a few words, remaining always within the bounds of the law.

"Can I have your name please?" He brought the camera into view, knowing full well that the sight of it would stimulate self-interest in its source.

Aggie readily responded, spelling her name in full in her best English.

"Am I right in assuming you are a Miss?"

"Yes, that's quite correct. I've lived here all my life".

"Indeed", he hastily stemmed a flow of the woman's life history.

"Now, that is interesting", he lied. "Now, Miss Wishart, what can you tell me about this tragic affair?"

"Well the body was found in a ditch near to the farm road".

"And, do you know who found the body Miss Wishart?"

"Oh, aye, I mean yes, it was Donald".

"Donald?"

"Aye, Donald McKay. He's an awfu' nice laddie. He's winchin' Monica".

"Monica?"

"Aye, ye see Moncia's Dave's dochter".

"Dave?"

"Aye, Dave Anderson, he's the farm manager".

"I see, now that is very helpful Miss Wishart. Now, I wonder if I could possibly ask you to pose for me?"

Aggie was instantly in her favourite posture with that hand on her hip.

She was, of course, unaware that Campbell had no intention of taking her photograph. He was simply going through the motions. The film in his camera had much more important images to receive.

There was obviously no point in continuing this session with the talkative Miss Wishart and Campbell retreated with all the grace and appreciative gestures he knew would be expected.

The incident had attracted the attention of the newspapers and, of course, the police. The news had also been communicated to the manor.

The Laird relied on McKenzie, his faithful gamekeeper to keep him up-to-date with what was going on in the area.

The general factotum was restricted to one visit each week. He had to report every Sunday morning at ten.

The time allocated was reserved for the affairs of the estate, and as the gamekeeper he made his weekly report that morning, is was with undisguised annoyance that the aristocrat saw the man approach the house.

McKenzie's report in the morning had been kept to the minimum required. He knew from previous experience that any unnecessary elaboration of detail would be angrily and abruptly curtailed by the intolerant master of the land, who had the habit of whipping his leg with his riding crop to emphasise his mood and his insistence on being told the bare necessities.

"Out with it man. Cut it short. Don't waste my time".

The reward for the faithful servant, who never failed his master, and upon whom the self same master relied for all the matters concerning the running of the estate.

The encounter occurred at the main door. McKenzie was not allowed to pass through the entrance reserved for the elite.

"Well, has your memory failed you? Is there something you have forgotten to tell me this morning?"

McKenzie was quite accustomed to this kind of treatment and had learned to ignore it. He never allowed his feelings to escape his mask of servitude and made his customary semblance by slightly raising his right hand.

"It's something else I think ye should ken aboot".

"Yes, well what is it?"

"A body has been found near ti the village".

"A body. You mean someone has died. I don't want to hear about people dying".

"No, not quite. Ye see, the lassie has been murdered".

"Well, no doubt, the police will be able to deal with the matter".

Without another word, McKenzie found himself alone on the massive doorstep of the manor.

Until he had the report of the post mortem and forensic tests, the Inspector had time to spend gathering information. Other members of the team were visiting all the residents and making records of each item for future reference.

He and D.C. Penman were now on their way to the mansion. The residence of the Laird, the Honourable James Harper-Nelson.

The Craigmire Estate covered an extensive area surrounded by the familiar high stone wall, which in turn enclosed the shroud of trees which served the aristocracy in their pursuit of privacy and escape from prying eyes.

The locals called the mansion "The Big Hoose' and their description was fairly accurate.

When the Inspector and D.C Penman finally reached the frontage they were astonished.

There was evidence of neglect everywhere. The centre section of the house was flanked by an east and west wing, providing space within the stone walls for thirty rooms.

Ivy grew rampant upwards past the two storeys and over the guttering. Weeds had been allowed to grow past the windowsills on the ground floor, whilst the tall, sightless windows, uncurtained and sinister in the silence, added to the feeling the two men had of unease as they sensed the odd atmosphere.

A huge, studded door, made in two halves discouraged any thought of gaining entry without an invitation from within.

With great difficulty, D.C Penman pulled the chain at the side of the doorway, causing a bell to sound deep inside the great house.

Several minutes elapsed before the jingling of keys timed to the sound of footsteps signalled the approach of someone from within.

Martha Heslop took the two men by surprise as she partly open a panel in the heavy, studded door.

Tall, dressed entirely in black, her hair combed straight back over her ears to form the traditional "bun' at the back, she stood in silence looking straight ahead as if the men didn't exist. She didn't speak.

"Good evening, I am Inspector Gilmour and this is Detective Constable Penman". We are investigating an incident which has occurred in the area and I wish to speak to the Laird".

"The master is not at home". The voice was affected by a certain air of authority. This woman was obviously a difficult person to deal with.

"Have you any idea when your master will be available?" The Inspector persisted.

"I have no idea". "I do not know the master's ways". The answer was short and abrupt and the voice was deep and hollow.

The panel in the doorway was closed and the two men were left facing each other in disbelief. It was obvious that the Laird would have to be interviewed and that seemed to be next on the cards.

The minister who was the Chairman of the Parish Council used his authority to grant the police use of the annex to the village hall as a control point.

The fixing of the temporary telephone line gave the local residents something else to add to their list of events.

Dick Hamilton was waiting for the Inspector and busied himself writing his report.

A point of interest caught the Inspector's eye. Dick had mentioned his talk with the "Hermit'. One named Hendry Ashford.

The word "hermit' fired the imagination with old men with beards. Eccentrics. Mysterious characters and all kinds of descriptions of a person who would choose isolation from society.

P.C Hamilton explained in detail that Hendry Ashford was not an "odd ball', but rather an ordinary kind of human being who lived alone.

The hermit's story was retold that day.

About a year previously, he had arrived to take up residence in the cottage rented from the Laird. To live with his young and attractive bride, Susan.

They had just been married.

A few days after the arrival of the newlyweds, the young bride disappeared and no-one had ever been able to trace her since.

It was natural that the young man would do everything in his power to find the truth.

All this was on police records and was eventually confirmed when the Inspector returned to headquarters.

The Inspector found a deluge of paperwork on his desk in the control. Written reports on the door-to-door enquiries. Names, addresses, occupations, missing persons.

He had delegated two officers to separate the items into various categories such as, for instance, rape, sex-offenders, burglary offences, etc.

Preliminary findings on the body established that the victim had been restrained by chains around her ankles and wrists, and that she had been sexually abused.

The Arm of the Law now seemed to require to be extended far beyond the immediate vicinity of the village. Any known associate of the dead girl would have to be found. She had been about sixteen years of age.

Her hands were unblemished, suggesting that she had not been a manual worker and could have been a student.

Significantly, she had taken wine before she died.

CHAPTER FOUR

Lizzie Duncan believed in presenting a good image to her customers, changing her white apron frequently during the day was part of the routine of keeping shop. After all; it was now afternoon and the apron just had to be changed.

The tapes, passing around her waist, completed her immaculate appearance in a bow and, to do the lady credit, she managed to maintain her rear as smartly as her front.

Now she was prepared to welcome the next caller who would ring that little bell above the shop door.

Lizzie Duncan had also the ability, known to many shopkeepers, to adjust her facial muscles into the semblance of a smile. A smile which the majority of the public accepted as genuine.

Lizzie's smile accounted for much of her popularity and trade.

There were occasions, however, when the "smile' failed to reach her eyes and it was given only to those who knew the woman well to suspect that the storekeeper's smile was perhaps a little transparent.

A visit by Mira, the minister's niece was a surprise.

The attractive brunette seldom ventured down from the manse when she paid her uncle a visit. Indeed, her visits were few and far between simply because she was not on very good terms with the lady of the manse.

The rather rigid attitude of her aunt didn't entirely meet with her approval.

There might well have been an element of jealousy behind the older woman's behaviour.

Whilst Mira had qualified as a school teacher, Mrs Davidson remained noticeably silent when the question of academic qualifications cropped up and she rarely participated in a conversation which required a higher level of knowledge.

Lizzie was ready with her smile. In fact, Lizzie, alike so many others, had a special smile for those she considered to be "better off' and, as the minister's niece, the young lady qualified for the special "smile' reserved for the "elite'. "Well, well. Miss Davidson. We don't often see you in these parts. Visiting your aunt and uncle?"

"Yes, we do like to keep in touch, Lizzie".

"You will have heard aboot these awfa' murders, the poor lassies, whit a shame".

"Yes we did hear about the tragic discovery of the young girl's body. It goes to show doesn't it. We never know what can happen these days".

Mira bought some groceries and made to leave.

Hendry Ashford passed her in the doorway as he was about the enter the store. He nodded and moved into the shop. Lizzie, ever watchful, concealed her interest in the young man's reaction. "There's something going on there" was the unspoken thought behind the deceptive smile.

Hendry approached the counter. "Just popped in for something for the tea".

Lizzie couldn't resist it. "Did you see the ministers niece?"

"Yes, Lizzie, as a matter of fact, I did notice her. She's a lovely girl".

That did it. It made Lizzie's day. To hear the "Hermit' describe a young lady as "a lovely girl'. Now that was something to pass on.

Just the kind of compliment Lizzie wanted to hear; especially from the   man who, for so long, had kept a close guard on his emotion.

Lizzie   also noted that the young man's unusually hasty departure and how he   stood   for   a   moment watching the minister's niece walk away towards the manse. Hendry was only too well aware of the unseen threat   to   vulnerable   young   women   in   the neighbourhood and his natural concern to the fact that Mira was travelling alone.

Without hesitation, he followed, deciding to keep a discreet distance between the girl and himself.

He was conscious of the fact that they had not been formally introduced and above all else, he found difficulty in directing attention towards other young women. It could be that he would never recover from the deep rooted sense of grief he lived with day after day.

Mira reached the green door in the wall at the manse and passed out of sight.

Hendry turned about and made his way home. It would be bacon and eggs for tea.

He was tidying the kitchen when the knock was heard on the door.

The Re. Mathew Davidson was on the door step. The minister wasn't smiling.

"Mr Ashford, am I given to understand that you followed my niece from the village to the manse?

Hendry noted the challenge in his voice. This was not merely a question. It was indeed a challenge. But why?

"You understand correctly. I certainly followed your niece to the manse".

"Are you aware that you caused her to be very upset. Now I want an explanation. What the devil do you think you were up to?" Hendry stood facing the clergyman and shook his head.

"I don't suppose for one minute it could have occurred to you that my intentions were purely honourable and that I was simply concerned for your niece's safety. I followed her at a discreet distance and when I saw her reach the gateway to the manse I made my way home".

"There is so much going about, these days, and one can't take any chances but, on the other hand, if this is the case, as you say, that you were concerned for the girl's safety, then I must apologise. However, you will understand that is necessary that the police should be told about this incident and you will have the opportunity to explain your actions to them".

With that said the man of "The Cloth' left the Ashford homestead.

Hendry hesitated. He knew that it was his duty to let the Inspector know.

He would "get his oar' in first.

He had little difficulty locating the Inspector.

Reg, was fully occupied with paper work and the Control was buzzing with activity. "Mr Ashford? Yes, I believe that I have heard your name mentioned. Now, what can I do for you?"

"I'm sorry to interrupt your work, Inspector, but something has arisen and I want to let you know my version of the events".

"Go ahead. I'm always willing to listen to what people have to say. After all; that's how we gather our information". Hendry related the events of the afternoon when he had escorted Mira to the manse. Emphasising that he had deliberately stayed will back from the young lady so as not to embarrass her and how he had been accosted by the minister who appeared to have been given the impression that the young man was stalking his niece on her way home to the manse.

He concluded. "A simple act of chivalry, Inspector, and I find myself under suspicion. A situation I want to avoid. Especially in these troubled times".

"Now, perhaps you are jumping to conclusions, Mr Ashford. The minister is probably on edge and a little over anxious".

"I happen to know that you are not the kind of man who would be going around, leaving bodies in ditches".

"However, thank you for calling in and letting me know what happened and now, if what you say is correct, we can expect the reverend at any time".

Hendry had the feeling that his actions would be the means of drawing unwelcomed attention to his movements and isolating himself, by choice, from the gossiping locals. He knew instinctively that what he had done and how it was to be interpreted would cause a lot of idle tongues to wag.

As expected, the minister was on his way to the police control.

The two men passed each other and, judging by the dark looks he received from the minister. Hendry was left in no doubt about the man's intentions.

On reflection, he accepted that Mira may have had the impression that she was being followed from the village to the manse and he knew that he must take the first opportunity to talk to the girl and to lay her mind at rest.

It was obvious that she had reached the manse in a distressed condition and that her uncle had reacted accordingly.

Mira was not a stranger in the village. He had seen her on several occasions when she had called in at the manse. She was bound to have known him. She must have heard about his tragic loss and how he lived alone with his grief.

The question was; Why had she panicked?

After all, he hadn't conducted himself in a manner which could have been misunderstood. Indeed, he had deliberately maintained a reasonable distance simply to avoid any possibility of embarrassing the young lady.

When the minister emerged from the police control he appeared to be deep in thought.

Hendry approached him.

Uppermost in his mind was the feeling that the minister had failed to allow him to fully explain the conditions related to his escorting Mira to the manse.

"If you have a moment Mathew".

"Mathew? Did the man actually address the Parish Minister by his first name? The minister's first reaction to this familiarity was evidenced by the stern expression and an outward thrust of the chin, emphasised by a petulant striking of the roadway with his cane. After all, the Parish minister had to maintain a certain dignity and the peasants had to be reminded from time to time.

"Mathew indeed".

Hendry persisted. "I feel that you and I must have a little talk about today's events. You haven't given me the opportunity to explain exactly how your niece arrived at the manse in a state of distress.

"I have carried out my duty and have informed the police and there is nothing to add to what has been said".

"Come on now, Mathew"

There it was again. It was enough. The Reverend Mathew Davidson, M.A. could not tolerate such an open disregard for his social status.

Showing obvious signs of his anger, he strutted away.

After all; even men of "The Cloth' can reach the limit of indifference.

The village of Craigmire was little different from any other Scottish community. The doors with no names. Men congregating at the village re-telling their favourite yarns and looking upon a world which bore little hope for them as they languished in their enforced inactivity.

Men, who, in their innocence, were blissfully unaware that, in secret places, pin-stipped individuals were scheming and plotting and planning the inevitable World War Two. A war which would be the means of causing the meeting place at the village well to be deserted. Where weeds would grow on earth trodden by many feet of men unceremoniously conscripted into service "for their King and Country' when, in so many cases, to certain death; never to return to their chatter and their laughter. The tales they told so many times; forgotten; a vacant space where only memories would keep the past alive.

Those who remained in the village would look towards that well and remember.

Lizzie Duncan's little bell above the door tinkling as the door opened and closed to a regular flow of customers and the "Bush Telegraph'.

A town dweller might live opposite a door on a landing for years and be totally unaware of the name of his neighbour but, in the country.

In the village without names, everyone knew everyone. They knew the family history down to the last arrival and much more besides.

There was the "Bush Telegraph'.

A phenomenon which existed then persists to this day.

No one can tell how much information is conveyed from one person to another; usually with the speed of light; but there is no denying the existence of the ability of the human species to communicate one with the other; to pass on information, trivial or serious, and where the actual source is vague and in most cases unfathomable.

Everyone knew about the encounter involving Hendry and the minister. They knew all the details and much more besides. Simply by reason of the fact that, in the repeated telling of the story, the story embellished and matured in accordance with the creative ability of the individual concerned.

The incident was now well out of proportion to the truth and Hendry found himself the target of abuse and ridicule.

He was the object of suspicion.

The men at the well muttered as he passed and former friends looked the other way.

Old Sammy Bogie who sat at his doorway on a wooden stool, playing jigs and reels on his melodeon, stopped playing and Lizzie Duncan had no smile on her face when she served the man who was alleged to have stalked the minister's niece home to the manse.

The "togetherness' which characterised the society of the village had rejected the man who had was mistakenly accused.

Hendry had never experienced such a serious situation.

Everyone had accepted him as part of the scene up to this time.

If only he could communicate with them. Tell them the truth. What he had intended to do when he escorted the young lady to her home. Even from a distance.

He had done nothing to be ashamed of. On the contrary; he ought to have been applauded for an act of chivalry, instead of being ostracised by people who were considered to be his friends.

It was obvious to the man that he would not be able to reason with the residents of the village when their attitude had obviously been instigated by the minister or his wife.

He decided to seek refuge in his cottage,

He hadn't the time to prepare a meal when the sound of voices outside alerted him to the gathering crowd shouting and threatening and obviously mis-informed.

Jockie Scott the "Giant Killer' was in the front of the crowd. Men and women who had been so friendly and were now showing their indignation at what they believed to be an offence.

Angry voices shouted abuse and there was a loud hammering on the front door.

Donald McKay heard the commotion. He too, had listened to the wagging tongues and it didn't take him long to realise that Hendry was in trouble.

He pushed his way through the crowd and turned to face them.

Donald was a sturdy lad and it was doubtful if anyone present would have tried to take him on.

He called for silence and held up both hands. He knew that there would have to be some kind of order before justice could be seen to be done.

It somehow appeared to be necessary to question those gathered at the cottage in such a rage. They would have to account for their behaviour. Why were they accusing the man who had been their friend for so long. Were they ready to condemn him without first hearing what he had to say?

Indeed, Hendry had nothing to answer for. What was he accused of? Donald shouted until he was hoarse but finally, the crowd began to listen to what he had to say.

"Listen everybody, there's nae need for a' this nonsense, You and I have kent Hendry Ashford for a long time and ye ken fine that he wouldna' dae the lass any harm.

"He followed her hame" shouted Jockie Scott.

"That's no quite true, Jockie, Hendry wiz only concerned aboot the safety o' the minister's niece, he didna' gan near her."

"The lassie wiz frantic when she got into the manse," shouted someone at the rear of the crowd.

Donald had heard the story and he couldn't believe that his friend would harm anyone.

"We havna' heard the true story" He shouted. "Let's hear whit Hendry has ti say" "Aye, that's right, get him oot here and let him tell his side o' the story."

The villagers were unanimous. They all wanted to hear what Hendry would say, Donald noted that the air had cooled considerably since he had at first intervened.

He walked slowly to the cottage door and knocked.

"Hendry, it's Donald, we want ti speak to ye"

Hendry, it's Donald, We want ti speak to ye."

Hendry had heard it all. He was still amazed at the sudden change in the attitude of those who he considered to be his friends.

However, he recognised Donald and he knew the lad to be a reasonable ally and he opened the cottage door.

At first there was silence.

It was as if the villagers had suddenly realised their folly.

Donald took advantage of the moment.

"Here's the man ye a' accuse, dae ye think Hendry wid molest the minister's niece?"

Hendry stepped out and stood beside Donald. He raised his hand.

"If you want to accuse anyone, why not go to the manse? If anyone is to blame it's her uncle, the minister. He allowed the lassie ti gan doon ti the village on her own and this is nae place for any lass to be oot on her own. "But you followed her" shouted someone from the rear of the crowd.

Donald seized the opportunity.

"You are quite right, Hendry did the decent thing and made sure that Mira got home safely. Anyone of us here would have done the same thing, and, as Hendry says, why not ask the minister why he allowed his niece to venture oot on her own.

P.C. Hamilton arrived.

"Whit's goin' on here?" Jockie Scott seemed to be subdued. He realised that his actions, to say the least, had been a little hasty. He explained what happened at the cottage and what they had all heard. "Well now, it seems that ye have managed to sort things and I can only suggest that ye all get off home and leave the man in peace."

There was much talk amongst the villagers as they followed the policeman's advice and made their way home.

Donald remained with his friend Hendry for a while and talked the whole affair over.

It was later that Aggie Wishart was able to throw some light on the matter when she disclosed that she had spoken to Mrs Davidson.

It was Mrs Davidson who had urged her husband to visit Hendry and, in some way, satisfy that strange quirk in human nature to stir trouble.

There are no words to adequately describe the mental torture and pain when we are facing the grim reality of the loss of one we love.

More so, as in the case of Hendry Ashford, there was the additional bitter element of uncertainty attached to the grief of absence.

The uncertainty. The anguish. The speculation and the un-answered questions associated with the sudden disappearance of a loved one.

The sudden loneliness experienced living in home he had prepared for his young bride. A home where he constantly looked for the reminders of her presence.

Her charm and her personality.

She was not in her favourite chair. Reading; knitting; sewing and doing the many things she was so capable of doing.

The house was silent, he couldn't hear her voice. The sounds remained only in the hollow of his mind.

When he found the courage to emerge to face the world again he found difficulty in adjusting to the kindly gestures of the people of the village who shared his deep sorrow and tried, in their own peculiar fashion, to help their friend.

We hear it said that "Time will heal' but we all know, only too well, that "Time' cannot erase our memory.

The memories Hendry cherished were clearly defined and had been so until he had seen the Minister's niece.

The attractive young lady had kindled a glow within him and he instinctively attempted to blur the image she had impressed on his mind.

It was Saturday and Hendry usually made a weekly visit to town and looked forward to his "high tea' in Porter's restaurant.

The tea house attracted customers in many ways apart from the excellent food. The wholesome aroma drifting along the pavement outside was temptation enough to lure the hungry into the well appointed interior.

He found his favourite table by the window where he could look down on the busy street where traffic and pedestrians performed the daily miracle of avoiding a collision and the continuous alignment of shops cast their glow over the scene with its limitless variety of odours. The fish and the fruit and the bakery or the grocery each and every one contributing to the way of life of the towns-people.

Hendry couldn't resist the lure of Porter's Tea Rooms. He had acquired the habit of popping in for a "High tea'. His favourite table was available and he settled into his usual chair by the window from where he could view the busy scene below.

Janet, a trim eighteen year old waitress, was forever alert and standing by his side with that infectious smile and an eyebrow raised which indicated to a regular like Hendry that she was ready to take his order. In Hendry's case, this was merely a gesture as Janet knew she would receive the same old order; Hendry's favourite; "The fish tea'.

It was good to sit down to a meal he hadn't cooked himself and to have it served by such an attractive young lady and not have the drudgery of washing up.

Fate must have been playing a hand on the particular occasion. Mira was seated at a table on the other side of the room. She was in conversation with a man and seemed to Hendry to be really enjoying herself.

He was suddenly conscious of a strange feeling of resentment at the sight of the young girl in the company of a man.

Strange; because he kept the memory of his wife close to his heart and had never abandoned hope that, some day, they would meet again.

He tried in vain to erase the image Mira had impressed on his mind but somehow her charm was stronger than his will to reject her.

He found himself watching the young couple and experienced a feeling of guilt. After all, he reasoned with himself, Mira was perfectly entitled to have the attentions of another man and, his last encounter with her had not been friendly. The feelings he experienced overcame his normal caution. He felt that he needed to talk to her. To explain the true nature of his intentions when he had been so unfairly accused of causing her to be alarmed. The inner conflict persisted. The effect Mira was having on his emotions was contrasted by the memories so deeply entrenched in his being. If only he could talk to the girl. Make her understand but; should he? Would he be unfaithful to the memory? He recognised the possibility that he might be ignored or totally rejected if he attempted to make any kind of advance. That chance encounter in the tea room had given him much to think about.

He found himself reviewing his past life and, for the first time since his great loss, he was projecting his thoughts into the future; where previously he had virtually been living in the past.

Where was he going. What was he to do with his life. Was it to be a life of loneliness for him? Yes; Mira had switched the controls from "Auto-pilot' to "Manual'. He was in the process of emerging from a state of introversion, allowing circumstances to follow a random course and, without the aid of "group therapy' the man began to examine his conscience. To adjust to his inner feelings and to include another girl in his world of fantasy.

Then again; he mused, if she accepted his attention, would he find himself comparing one image with another. Habit with habit, personality with personality. Would he be able to cope with this dilemma. Could he allow another image to invade the inner sanctum he had preserved for so long.

A rural community thrives on gossip. Any item of news can be instrumental in breaking the spell of monotony. Aggie Wishart the middle aged spinster could be relied upon to offer her contribution to the daily round of chatter and the villagers looked forward to meeting the teller of tales. She seldom failed to amaze them with her ability to tap the lines of communication. Aggie's latest "bulletin' reached the peak of the spinster's reputation. She passed from door to door almost as if she were the "Town Cryer' broadcasting the latest news.

Now that Mira, the minister's niece, was to be the new infant teacher at the village school, following the retirement of Mrs Blakey who would be remembered by many grown ups for her stern yet kindly mannerisms. Margaret Blakey had certainly left her "Footprints on the Sands of Time' in that little village school and her replacement, Mira, would find it difficult to make her own impression; fulfilling the role as the school teacher who would be remembered by successive generations as "The lady who was in charge' on their eventful first day at school.

Hendry Ashford had almost given up hope of meeting the girl who had become the object of his attention.

This latest development offered new possibilities; new hope, which revived the "Yes, No' conflict churning away in his heart.

It was with an air of optimism that he looked forward to the occasion when he would come face to face with the young lady who had broken the guard around his heart.

The village hall played a major role in the social life of the community. Especially when the sound of laughter and music filled the evening air. The clamour and the gaiety signalled the gateway of escape from the toils and responsibilities of everyday life.

Hendry seldom ventured forth to share the weekly revelry with the locals. The reels and the Strathspeys and the cosy waltzes as well as the heavy smoke laden atmosphere and the hiss of oil lamps suspended overhead. Now it appeared that recent events had had an effect on the "Hermit'.

He decided to go the Dance.

Habitually well dressed, he spent more time than he usually did, with his preparations for a night out.

He knew the locals well. He knew that he would be subject of looks and glances by the men and women. The scrutiny usually given to strangers.

He bought a ticket and passed through the doorway to join the crowd dressed in shirts bearing the unmistakable signs of sweat under the armpits.

A dance was in progress and groups were spiralling a circuit around the hall. Shouting and raising their arms aloft in the traditional form of the Scottish dance. She was there. She was with a formation swinging and swirling and following the intricate movements with ease.

His heart told him more than his mind could tell. His heartbeat had increased at the sight of the beautiful minister's niece.

A final clash of symbols marked the end of the noise and clamour of the dance and the walls of the hall were, once again, lined, with ladies on one side and the lads on the other side.

Hendry was glad and releaved to see Donald MacKay.

Donald smiled and moved along to make room for his friend.

"Someone's lookin' awfa' smart tonight", he joked.

Hendry nodded and straightened his tie nervously and then he had an idea. Perhaps Donald would help him. Donald could tell Mira that he wished to speak to her. To dance with her. Donald could "test the waters', so to speak.

Donald readily agreed and somehow he sensed Hendry's interest was more that he cared to admit.

He was glad to know that his friend had found something new to do and to think about. Sharing an interest in the opposite sex?

"Take your partners for the St. Bernard's Waltz" bawled the Master of Ceremonies, who happened to be the school master.

Donald glided smoothly across the floor and claimed Mira as his partner. She rose, smiling, and placed her arms discretely around the grinning blacksmith. As they danced, Donald didn't hesitate to convey the message he had been entrusted with. "Have you noticed that Hendry Ashford is here tonight, Mira?" "Yes, I did notice him, Donald. He's looking very smart too."

If telepathy exists then it was at work with Mira.

She saw Hendry seated against the wall. Alone. She could hear his heart beating and could sense the confusion in his mind.

She noted how tense he was and how he watched the dancers enjoying themselves.

"I'm sorry, Donald, I know now that Hendry was concerned for my safety when I walked to the manse."

Donald gave his partner a friendly squeeze.

She didn't object.

She liked Donald and somehow it was beginning to dawn on her that she liked Hendry too.

As they danced towards Hendry, Donald grabbed his friend and pulled him to his feet.

Before he knew what had happened, Hendry was facing this wonderful girl and she had her arms around him. They were dancing. He was in a trance.

She was extremely considerate. She knew the torment her dancing partner was going through. Now she had the opportunity to put the record straight.

"Hendry, I'm, so sorry that you were victimised the other day. I now know that you were concerned for my safety and my uncle rather foolishly acted without reason. Hendry could hardly speak. He had had no time to prepare for this sudden close encounter with this young woman. He couldn't find the words he wanted to say.

"I am so glad, Miss Davidson. As you rightly say, I was concerned for your safety"

"Yes, and what did you get in return?"

"The villagers were a little hasty with their accusations, but it all came right in the end."

"By the way, Hendry, Please call me Mira, I dislike formalities. Friends?"

Hendry smiled and swept his partner around the floor. He was experiencing a surge of excitement we all know so well when we are faced with the problem of gender. He was not accustomed to the near proximity of the female form. After all; it was now about a year since he had had physical contact with a member of the opposite sex; and Mira. Especially

Mira. Well this was an unforeseen attack on his reserves.

Mira was radiant. Flowing, naturally waved hair crowning her attractive features. Being so close to each other set the "chemicals' into action. They were both responding to that awakening of their natural instincts and desire.

The warmth of the soft light of the oil lamps overhead. The music and the rhythm. The "magic' of the dance of love.

It was happening and they both knew it and, as dance followed dance, Hendry claimed Mira at every opportunity and the locals nudged each other and nodded. They were witnesses to what was going on between the "Hermit' and the Minister's niece.

Hendry suddenly recalled the scene in the tea-room. Was he intruding? He knew that, before he could make any advance, he should be certain that Mira was free to make a choice.

"Have you a boyfriend, Mira?"

Mira laughed. "I know what you are thinking Hendry. You saw me in the tea-room the other day, No I haven't a boyfriend, that was just a casual acquaintance." She saw relief on his face.

Then, boldly. "Mira, if I ask you to allow me to see you home tonight, will you say yes?"

"Of course, Hendry, my goodness, we have practically spent the entire evening in each others arms and we might as well complete the evening by sharing the roadway home."

The effect was predictable. Hendry could have jumped and shouted with delight. The rigid past had been wiped from his system.

The last dance. The occasion when the boy finds the courage to ask the girl that vital question, "Can I see ye hame?'

Donald and Monica saw it all and they were glad to know that their friend had found someone who could break through the barrier in Hendry's life.

Hendry and Mira walked side by side. He hesitated for a while, wondering if any personal contact would be premature or even (heaven forbid) rejected. Mira solved the problem, she took his hand, he pressed her fingers and she responded.

It was a clear night and mild and they talked as they walked on their way to the manse.

Hand in hand? Well, at least this was a beginning.

He put his arm around her waist and, in response, she pressed her arm around him leaning inwards towards him; sensing his strength.

They were seen by the villagers as they walked slowly along the roadway. The "drums' would be beating tomorrow. Everyone would know that the Hermit had take Mira home.

Too soon; They reached the manse, now the moment of parting. Hendry faced another decision. Was it a case of a hand shake and a "pleasant goodnight?' or should he take her in his arms and find those lips he had been longing to kiss? This was indeed the moment of truth. It would be all or nothing.

He stood facing her. Mankind has long since lost that sensitivity, that illusive instinctive recognition of emotion; the feeling; a knowledge that one or the other has been affected by radiance; unseen; but nevertheless existent and irresistible. Coded signals, long since ignored by the human race stimulating a mutual desire to share the fragrance of the intimate contact of lip to lip. She pressed her body closer and her arms tightened around his neck. She could feel the pounding of his heart against her breasts.

Goodnight kiss. The ecstasy they shared sealed a relationship and confirmed what had no need for the spoken words. Affection and love.

He knew that he would have to move away but he seemed to be paralysed. Fixed to the spot. Revelling in every moment of this embrace of love.

She stood back and turned to move away. Being separate, was, to each, a new and painful event in their newly found affection for each other.

"Goodnight, Hendry" and she was gone.

He stood for a while regaining his composure, then set out for his cottage home. Mrs Davidson was waiting for her niece and at that moment, she was not aware that Mira had been accompanied home by Hendry Ashford.

"Did you enjoy yourself dear?"

"Why, yes antie. There was a good crowd at the dance."

"Did the school master see you home?"

"No, I had another companion" Mira found herself chuckling within at the thoughts running through her mind when auntie received the truth.

"Other companion?"

"Oh yes indeed, he is a local lad. You know him. Hendry Ashford?"

"Hendry Ashford?" You mean to say that you allowed that horrid man to accompany you all the way home from the village? Mira, I really thought that you would have had more sense. Hendry Ashford. Huh!"

"Auntie, you are wrong in thinking that Hendry is not an honest and decent man. Mira continued, "It isn't fair to treat Hendry as if he were a criminal who had carried out the murder of his wife. She disappeared soon after they had arrived in the village. Hasn' he suffered enough?"

"Who is to say what the man is capable of doing? Did it occur to anyone that there is always the possibility that he married her for her money? Her death will always be a mystery."

"That is very unkind, Auntie, you should be ashamed to be harbouring thoughts like that about an innocent man."

"Have it your own way. I only hope that I am wrong, my lass. Auntie persisted. "Just remember what I have said"

She strutted off to awaken the long suffering minister of the Parish.

Aggie Wishart was the caretaker at the Parish church. She cleaned and she polished and she dusted the pews and she put the flowers in their vases and she listened. Aggie always listened.

She could hear the woodwork creaking and groaning at the changes in temperature. The wind in the bell tower at times, eerie, and spooky as it resonated inside the bell.

The Parish Minister was having a conversation with his wife in the rear hall. Aggie was listening.

Mrs Davidson was raving about the events of the previous evening and she repeated in detail every word spoken during her exchange with her niece.

"And we still don't know what happened to that man's wife when she suddenly disappeared. Just married and the next day she's gone; No trace; Nothing. Aggie couldn't complete her weekly tasks quickly enough. She simply had to rush to the village. She had to get all this off her chest.

What a sensation. The minister's wife suspecting Hendry Ashford of murdering his wife. This was the real "stuff'.

CHAPTER FIVE

An event, such as the sensational discovery of the girl's body in a small, rural, community is certain to open up cupboards where "skeletons' are secreted away. Like people all over the world, the local inhabitants of Craigmire knew, for certain, that everyone had a skeleton in a cupboard.

The time had come for some "bones' to be brought out for an airing. The oral tradition would not have it otherwise and in the "Plough' the regulars were enjoying their customary "resurrection' of tales, dead and buried, in the social history of the village.

Joe Penman had heard all the stories and, being the successful proprietor of the Plough, Joe agreed with everyone.

Aggie Wishart had cast her spell over the village and Lizzie Duncan had much more to talk about as she passed the goods over the counter.

Lizzie was convinced that Hendry Ashford was one "to keep an eye on'. His recently announced association with the minister's niece was surely cause for concern. She shared Mrs Davidson's talent for malicious gossip; after all; quoting Mrs Davidson "Just how did Hendry Ashford's wife disappear?" The mystery still remained whilst the villagers accepted the husband on friendly terms since his tragic loss.

No one could say how the young bride had been spirited away.

Yes, Aggie had successfully directed attention to Hendry Ashford and the "drums' began to roll.

Mira noted the looks as she made her way through the village. The heads inclined towards each other as whispers moved from ear to ear.

She was on her way to visit the object of so much attention and this possibility did not escape the watchful individuals as their excitement increased.

Hendry heard the knock on his door. It was unusually light. His heart leapt in his chest as he opened the door to see the girl who had occupied his thoughts and completely revived his natural instincts towards the opposite sex.

She smiled. "Arn't you going to invite a young lady in?"

"Yes, please come in" he stammered as he stood uncertainly aside to allow his charming visitor to pass into the cottage.

The "village drums' signalled the latest news. She had actually gone into the cottage. Hendry led the way as Mira looked around in amazement. The clean, fresh atmosphere not entirely to be associated with the living quarters of a solitary man where there would be ample evidence of the fallacy that the male of the species is incapable of keeping his abode in order.

"Hendry, my dear, What a delightful home you have"

Recalling their last loving embrace, Hendry took her hands and drew her towards him. How would she react to this advance. Would she resist? Would he be assuming too much?

Slowly she moved in acceptance of his unspoken invitation closing that space between their bodies. Their inner senses stirring the desire to relish the flavour of the love which had been so easily accepted by both.

She did not resist. Slowly, looking into her eyes, he knew that she felt the deep sense of love he felt for her and that her response was to surrender.

They stood together. Their bodies crying out to be touched; to revel in the sensation of contact one with the other. Their lips responded to that kiss which, love alone, can give. They were caught up in the spell of the mystery which may never be solved. Reluctantly, they stood apart and Mira began to look around the room.

Hendry was glad that he had previously removed all the photographs he had displayed for so long. It would have been slightly embarrassing for Mira to find so much attention being given to his wife. He now knew that this was in the past. He felt renewed and could see the future ahead of him for the first time since his loss.

Mira was not one to conceal the truth about how she felt.

"Have you any photographs of your wife, Hendry?"

This was an awkward moment. He would rather have avoided his new found love overlapping the past but he produced some photos and handed them to Mira. She looked at the young couple in the gilt frame. She saw that Hendry's wife had been an exceptionally beautiful girl and this served to add to the sympathy she felt for the man she had fallen in love with. "Hendry, she was a very pretty girl. I am so sorry and somehow I think I can share some of the grief you must have gone through."

"It's all over now, my dear. I have lived with the image long enough and you; He drew her towards him; You have changed my life completely with a kiss."

He put the photos in a drawer and placed his hands on her shoulder. "Come, I'll show you my den."

He led the way through a doorway at the rear of the cottage into a large workroom. Mira was impressed.

The room was full of drawing equipment and models of dwellings.

"Are you an architect, Hendry?"

"Yes" He indicated several parchments hanging on the walls.

Mira walked towards them and stood shaking her head in amazement.

"My goodness, Hendry, I had no idea that you were so highly qualified, do you work at this?"

"Sometimes, as a matter of fact, I do manage to keep the wolf from the door so to speak; by taking a commission or two. Now let's see the bedroom."

He led the way to another room. Even the bed had been made up. Everything was neat and tidy.

They were in each other's arms and there was no doubt in either of their minds that nature demanded only one conclusion.

Their bodies were craving for attention. Passionate and full in all of its rapture. The bed was inviting and all that they required.

All around the cottage. In the village with no names on the doors, there were faces at windows and little groups of "imaginative' neighbours creating all kinds of possibilities about what was going on behind the painted walls of Hendry's home.

If only they could have known.

Hendry and Mira did more than make love that day. They made a decision that was to be the cause of more activity on the "bush telegraph'

Mira, about to take over her appointment at the village school, had no hesitation in deciding to move in with Hendry and his immaculate little cottage. After all, living in the village would be a great advantage and they would be able to share their lives together despite the talk of the town.

Later, Hendry escorted Mira to the bus stop on the roadway to town and when they emerged from the cottage with its secrets; wasn't it surprising? There wasn't a villager in sight.

Aggie Wishart's view of the world around her was limited to the daily succession of events in the vicinity of the village where she had lived all of her life as a spinster. She belonged to that class of individuals who have been either unsuccessful in love or lack a natural inclination to share their lives with another person.

Consequently, her interests lay outwith her narrow field of view and concentrated on the behaviour and habits of others and it was inevitable that she had taken a keen interest in the mystery within the walls of Hendry's cottage.

Her feet could hardly touch the ground as she sped towards the manse. Mira and Hendry living together? The minister must be told. The young couple hadn't secreted their "skeleton' in a cupboard. Instead; with complete disregard for what was, in these days, acceptable and conventional behaviour; they hung their boney friend above the lintel of their abode for all to see, and in so doing, had much in common with those who rejected the liturgy and dogma and the hypocrisy of the "righteous' in our midst.

Mira's uncle was livid at the prospect of facing his parishioners with the "sin' of his niece hanging over his head.

Nation-wide; the question of immorality was kept under "wraps'. Rich and poor, alike, were divided into those who complied with "the code' and those who did not follow the guiding principles laid down in the "book of books'.

During these days the Institution of Marriage retained a degree of respect which has, in time, been progressively degraded.

Urged by his spouse, the minister had little alternative to quoting the scriptures and regaling the two "sinners' with all kinds of threats of "eternal damnation'. As far as Mira and Hendry were concerned, the minister might well have found other things to do. They ignored the preacher completely and, in time, the dust was finally allowed to settle and the young lovers lived their lives in peace.

CHAPTER SIX

Campbell was always one step ahead when it came to the sifting of news from the debris.

Whilst "the pack' stampeded around the village trying to write something in their notepads, he faded from view. His actions were borne through past experience, when his movements were watched by those who knew him and the methods he used to score the headlines.

He could have had plenty of company if the others had any idea that he was up to his old tricks; playing it alone.

The newsman had decided that it was time that he had a word with the elusive Laird.

His enquiries in the village had revealed the fact that the residents knew very little about the Landowner and his estate.

It was with great difficulty that he managed to leave the village and walk to the main road undetected. He had decided to walk to the mansion because, if he had approached his car, he would have been spotted and that was the last thing he wanted to happen at this time.

He followed the trail left by the Inspector and D.C. Penman some time earlier. On passing through the entrance to the drive he noted that the two gates sagged from their hinges on the stone pillars and that Nature, as if to apologise for her destruction of the once beautiful wrought iron work, shrouded her handiwork with the blooms of wild flowers and ferns.

The twisting drive seemed to be endless as he walked beneath the canopy of foliage, which occasionally allowed bright beams of sunlight to illuminate the shrubs in bloom and wild flowers revelling in their brief share of the solar rays. The bright light in striking contrast to the deep shadows of the undergrowth beyond.

His first view of the house didn't impress him. There was no laughter, no movement, no sound. Just as it had appeared to the two men who had previously visited the scene.

The mansion, with its tall, sightless windows, glared at him ominously. He felt ill at ease.

The huge, studded door was slightly open, yet no one answered his attempt to announce his arrival.

Silence can be more effective in creating that feeling of suspense than sound in all of its various forms.

He made his way back to the village but, as an afterthought, he turned towards the house and took several photographs. After all, they might come in handy later.

About one hundred yards from the house he passed what he knew to be the family crypt. This was obvious when the stonework and headstones were taken into consideration.

The gate was partly open. Not significant in itself, but the fact remained that the gate had recently been moved according to the state of the weeds which had been disturbed.

Broken twigs and crushed weeds led him inwards to a stone tomb.

The lid had obviously been moved and had not been replaced.

It was possible to see inside through a small gap between the edge of the lid and the walls of the tomb.

His heart leapt in his chest.

In the dark interior he could see a skeleton, and alongside the body of a young girl.

He too, experienced that odour of rotting flesh. It made him sick. A gleam on the finger of the skeleton caught his eye.

Reaching inwards towards the gruesome contents of the stone covered in moss, he recovered two rings from the bony finger.

Campbell photographed the scene and left the crypt.

He was nearing the lodge gates when, out of the shrubbery, the challenge. "Whit are ye doin' here?"

He could see no one.

Again the voice, coarse and menacing, "Did ye hear me, whit are ye doing' here?"

A huge man stepped on to the drive as if from nowhere. His rugged, weather-beaten complexion seemed to match his demeanour. Twin-barrels of a shotgun said it all. Campbell had lost this round. There was no point in arguing with the likelihood of being on the receiving end of two rounds of lead shot.

He had come face to face with the gamekeeper. The rent collector, the factor, the general handyman. The man who, alone, had dealings with the man of mystery, the Laird.

Campbell thought it prudent to make some kind of explanation.

"I am a reporter with The Times, and I wanted to have a word with the Laird. It's my duty as a newsman to keep the public abreast with all the news."

"Ye've the gift o' the gab, for sure. Noo, let me tell ye whit my duty is. Ye see, it's my duty to keep buggers like you oot."

There was no mistaking the man's intention.

Campbell made as dignified a retreat as he could muster, pointing that camera in the direction of this rugged individual, and pulling the trigger in the hop that he had captured another contribution to the file on the Craigmire mystery.

The high stone wall surrounding the estate marked the edge of the roadway leading back to the village.

The care and attention lavished on the area by former generations had long since, been abandoned. Where there had been evidence of careful pruning on the hedge rows and pathways free from the intrusion of weeds, there was now a profusion of weeds finding their roots in every nook and cranny, and, if the truth would be permitted, the summertime blooms did much to enhance the otherwise derelict appearance of the once magnificent residence of the family Harper-Nelson.

Campbell walked back to the village admiring the colourful splendour. His mind churning over all the confusing details he had gathered so far in his quest for news.

It occurred to the newsman that somewhere in the vicinity there must be someone who knew more than they were telling. There must be someone who had seen some unusual movements and behaviour and, all things considered, Campbell was aware of the awful truth of the fact that he was dealing with the death of a young girl. A death which had been caused under the most terrible circumstances.

Reasoning and logic would eventually produce some results. It was merely a matter of patient sifting of the known facts and forming a fair conclusion on the merits of the evidence produced.

Then he heard the voices.

Voices raised in anger. Unseen in the seclusion of the estate. A cultured voice; surely that of the Laird and the voice of one who had not benefited from the training enjoyed by the more fortunate in our midst. "You bloody fool; leaving the body in that ditch. Surely you must have known that it would be found and now look what you have started. What is going to happen to us if they ever find out how the body got there?"

"The gravedigger hadna' dug the hole deep enough. I couldna' dae any diggin' because it would have been noticed and where would we be then?"

"That's why I had ti dump the lassie in the ditch"

"You know damned well what you were doing, you silly bugger, it has always worked in the past. You should have made sure that the body wouldn't be found. You don't think for one minute that I am going to fork out cash to a blundering idiot who cannot do his job properly?"

Then silence and the Campbell knew that this exciting dialogue had ended. He was no faced with the problem of piecing together the fragments of information he had heard over the stone wall.

It was obvious that the cultured one had been paying for the removal and disposal of bodies and that the fact that a girl's remains had been discovered in the ditch near to the village had been a gross mistake.

His duty was obvious. He must report all that had occurred to the Police.

This was indeed vital information and a positive link with the persons involved in the killing of innocent victims.

He was confident that he would be able to identify the owner of the uneducated voice he had heard over the wall, and, his experience of years dealing with all kinds of characters left him in no doubt that when he met the owner of that voice he would be able to place him as the man who had admitted his guilt in the murders.

D.C. Penman was in the control in the village hall annex. He listened with great interest into what the newsman had to say.

He too shared the delight in this breakthrough and it now appeared to be vital that his superiors should be up-dated with the news.

The two men left the control and were making their way through the village when Blyth appeared. He had come from the direction of the main road. The same route taken by Campbell.

There was something about the man's behaviour that attracted attention.

Campbell recalled how Police on duty at a Naval Dockyard had talked about the effect of guilt on a person.

They claimed that they were able to spot the one with the hidden loot simply by his odd behaviour. Faltering footsteps. Inordinate attention to insignificant objects. An exaggerated attempt by the guilty to look innocent. It all showed itself to the trained observer.

Campbell lacked the expertise of the Police but had had sufficient dealing with the public to note the unusual behaviour of the man with the broken nose. Blyth hadn't the intelligence to put on a convincing act and to avoid being conspicuous and, as he walked passed the two men, he looked pathetically under stress. "Guilt' was written all over his face.

Penman looked enquiringly at Campbell. "Where has that one come from?"

"That's Blyth, and he must have come from the estate."

"Could he be the man you heard talking over the wall?"

"There is only one way to find out. Let's have a word with him"

They approached Blyth and D.C. Penman, asked the man if he would care to go with them to the control.

Blyth's response betrayed what he must have been feeling, "I havna' done anything wrang."

"You are Mr Blyth? Yes? Well now Mr Blyth you have no need to be worried about talking to us."

"all we want to do is to ask you some questions and surely there can be no harm in that?"

"I ken you buggers. You twist everything a man has ti say. However, I have nothing to hide."

Blyth allowed himself to be led into the control room.

Penman moved to the seat behind his makeshift desk and sat down.

"Can you tell us where you have been during the last hour, Mr Blyth?"

Blyth's eyes were transparent. It was obvious that the man was frantically seeking an answer which would place him anywhere other than in the estate.

"I just went for a walk. Noo is there anything wrang wi' that?"

"No, indeed, Mr Blyth, in fact it is a very pleasant way to pass the time especially with this fine summer weather. Where did you go for your walk?"

D.C. Penman decided to disrupt the man's composure at this stage. To wade in and catch him off his guard.

"During your walk, you met the Laird and had a talk with him?"

This completely shattered Blyth's confidence. It was obvious that he had met the Laird secretly and that he had expected the meeting to be beyond the limits of prying eyes.

"The Laird? Oh aye, the Laird. Aye, the man just happened to be passin' by when I spoke to him."

Blyth looked at the two men expectantly. Somehow betraying the hope that his answer would be accepted in the casual context he had intended it to be.

Penman persisted.

"Inside the estate. Behind the wall. A secret meeting, Mr Blyth?"

"Who the hell told ye aboot that?"

"You can admit that you were talking to the Laird and we just happen to know what you were talking about."

At this point the Inspector arrived in the room and D.C. Penman rose to give his superior his chair.

The detective quickly recounted the events which had brought about this strange encounter with the man seated at the desk. Looking very much the worse for "wear'.

Placing both hands on his desk, the Inspector looked intently at Blyth. A man clearly disadvantaged and showing signs of total collapse of whatever defence his frugal mind could offer to these experts with their questions. He was completely unable to fabricate a plausible escape from the position he now found himself in.

"I didna' dae anythin' ti the lassies"

The man's defence had crumbled.

Taking advantage of this momentary lapse the Inspector probed deeper.

"Are you telling us that someone else killed the girl we found in the ditch. Do you have any idea who that might be? Who was the person who carried out these terrible crimes?"

"Ye better ask the Laird that question" Blyth's reply was non committal.

"You have known about these murders for some time, Mr Blyth, and you must have known that it was your duty to inform the Police."

At this stage the Inspector was faced with a dilemma. Had he sufficient evidence to justify detaining this man? Had he sufficient supportive material with which he could comply with the Law?

He decided to continue the interrogation and it was obvious that Campbell would be required to leave the room.

The Inspector was well aware of the reporters reputation for gathering the "fruity' details which added sense to sensation. As a matter of fact, Campbell was not too keen on being a witness to confessions or being personally involved in the material he dealt with on a daily basis.

Outside the village hall the locals were, for once, cheated out of the new developments in the Craigmire mystery. The locals went about their toils stoking their fires and causing the chimneys to send clouds of dark smoke into a cloudless sky.

Inspector Gilmour could see that the man seated before him was tense and afraid and taking into account the horrific nature of the crimes so dramatically discovered in the village such apprehension and caution on the part of one who found himself at the receiving end of these penetrating questions was quite understandable.

"Now, Mr Blyth, there is no need for you to be alarmed at this stage, after all, we havn't much to go on apart from the fact that you have made a statement implicating another person, in the murder of the girl found in the ditch. However, if you wish, you might tell us all you know about the incident and who you know is responsible for carrying out the crime.

I'm sure that you can be a great help to us in our enquiries."

Blyth sat in front of the Inspector, shaking his head. It could have been the sudden realisation of the responsibility he felt for what had occurred to end the life of an innocent young girl.

The truth that he had been an accomplice to the aristocrat who lived amid his priceless possessions in the luxury of the "Big Hoose'.

Despite the confusion in his mind, he was able to reason that the Police might be doubtful about the identity of the men in the estate and were using what they had said about the matter as a ploy to undermined his composure.

He knew the Police methods, he had had many dealings with the men in blue and he had learned a few tricks on the way.

Recollecting these previous "encounters' the man began to show signs of regaining his confidence.

"Am I under arrest?"

"No, Mr Blyth, you are not under arrest at the moment."

"So, I am free to go?"

"Yes, you are free to go. However, I have to warn you that in the light of what we have been discussing, you should not leave the vicinity of the village. Do you understand Mr Blyth?"

Blyth rose and left the control unaware of the little signals passing between the two detectives.

When he emerged into the summer air he paused and took a deep breath and made his way home.

CHAPTER SEVEN

Tom Bain, the foreman met Dave every morning and discussed the days work for the men. The two men worked well together, planning the rotation of crops and setting the time scale to suit the production of the crops.

There was also the husbandry of the dairy herd and the distribution of milk.

The forty milk cows maintained a steady flow of prime milk. A pedigree, freesian herd, distinctive in their black and white coats, furnished the landscape during the time when they were allowed to feed out-of-doors.

In winter, the animals were housed and attended to in the byre and this, in turn, produced a considerable quantity of manure.

It was the time of the year when all the sheds occupied by the animals during the winter months were cleared of manure and the men were ordered to carry out this somewhat odorous task. Working day-by-day with the animals they were accustomed to this kind of work and they were quite unaware of the smell of manure.

The ploughmen had a lifestyle which was distinctive from the living conditions of town dwellers.

They had a language of their own. Some of it unprintable.

They worked had and they lived hard. Especially on Saturday nights, when the "Plough' resounded to their bawdy songs.

Most of them knew nothing more that what they were asked to do.

Watch them as they ploughed the land. Note the pride with which they would turn their heads to assess the quality of the mark on the soil. Watch them as they would handle the teams of horses. These majestic, docile beasts of burden, the Clydesdales. Man and beast, working in perfect harmony.

Listen to their words of command. Brief and almost inaudible, yet obeyed without the slightest hesitation.

The ploughman's day began at about 4.30 a.m., when the stable door would be opened to release the unmistakable smell of ammonia and the warmth of the animals.

A chorus of deep throated grunts would welcome the turning of the stable door key and the lighting of the paraffin oil lamp. The great beasts would nod their heads in expectation of the morning ration of corn and hay.

Thus, the villagers saw the familiar cart loads of manure, steaming, even the warmth of the day, rocking and swaying over the rough surface of the main street through the village on their way to the storage site, where a large amount of the previous fertiliser would be stored for a year or more, depending upon the needs of the land.

Out in the edge of the field the hidden grew larger with each cartload, and a steady stream of carts passed to and from the farm.

The carters were quite unaware that the loads of manure which they were piling in the corner of the field would, one day, become a "Slow Cooker'.

They knew nothing about spontaneous combustion and the chemical reactions taking place within the mass.

The resultant steam, yet. They accepted this. It was only natural that the manure would give off steam.

Over a period of a few days, the farm buildings had been cleared and made ready with bedding of straw in preparation for winter housing of the animals.

The men loitering at the well watched the daily passage of cartloads of manure. It was part of the annual routine and was accepted as part of daily life in the village.

It was also quite natural for each member of the group to have formed his own opinion of the others. Every member was measured in terms of how he behaved and what he generally had to say.

There was, of course, a pecking order.

Relying on his build and reputation, Bill Blyth elected himself Top Dog in the pack. A condition accepted by the others in silence.

The five mile "bus journey to town restricted their movements and ambition to seek work. Denied the opportunity of full employment, over a prolonged period, these men had succumbed to a state of indifference and acceptance of their circumstances and had lost the incentive to work under the regularity and discipline demanded by full-time occupations.

The meagre payment from the Labour Exchange kept them on the verge of poverty and time spent with their cronies at the well relieved the strain of cramped conditions in their homes, where the women folks struggled with the physical burden associated with the cooking, washing and the rearing of the children.

The men had each a character with which he was known. The men who sat in silence. The "Listeners' and the "Talkers' and those who walked to and fro' aimlessly, as they talked about the matters which appealed to their limited intelligence.

For some unknown reason, it was considered to be manly to eject spit through the teeth. A filthy habit, displayed with pride by those who had accomplished the technique.

Blyth was a master at this practice as well as being fluent in unprintable language.

Strange as it may seem, bad language was stopped abruptly when a woman approached the well. Her presence there as she filled the buckets of water would be marked with silence or a dramatic change of subject.

It was Monday. Three days since the discovery of the body in the ditch.

It was the time of day when the school children were allowed out of doors to scream their delight and mill around their confined area at play.

A number of men had gathered at the well. Later, they would expect to be called in to have their midday meal.

They accepted the stranger who had joined them. In his casual dress, he was known to the men as one of the investigating team working on the murder case.

Blyth acted up to expectations.

"Are you lads getting any further wi' yer work on the murder?"

"There is always sure to be progress, no matter how trivial it may seem." Harry Bowman had long since discovered the effect of seeming to be forthright. Talking, but at the same time saying nothing.

"Have ye still nae idea who could have done it?"

Jockie Scott was a stocky built lad. He continued. "Let me get my hands on the bugger."

Blyth interrupted. Sniggering "You?, noo whit wid ye dae?"

Jockie moved close to the big man, who made the fatal mistake of underestimating the smaller man.

Jockie closed his fist and matched up as if to do battle,

No one saw Jockie move. His broad fist made contact with the big mans jaw and the Top Dog lay flat on the ground.

The detective didn't intervene and tried to conceal a smile. Mr "Big Mouth' had seemingly met his match.

The others assisted Blyth to his feet and he staggered away, obviously lacking any inclination to make any more of this encounter with the smaller man.

Jockie wiped his sweating palms on his trousers. "That bastard has been asking for that some time."

Now that Blyth had left and there was no longer any threat to them, the other men heartily agreed with Jockie. Blyth needed a fist on the jaw.

"Blyth's a bad bugger", Jockie remarked. "He spends too much time watching the bairns in the playground."

Harry was immediately alerted at this last remark. Any suggestion of pervertion relating to anyone was of the greatest importance.

Harry ventured, "Has this Blyth a child at the school?"

Jockie laughed. "Blyth! a bairn at the school? Naw, there's nae lass aboot here wid hae onything ti dae wi' that man."

Webster, an older man, puffing away at his clay pipe, asked "Did he no dae time for rapin' a lassie in the bushes?"

"Rape?". Now Harry was interested.

Jockie explained, "He got three years and he was lucky. Ye see, the lass had a bad reputation and that wiz takin' intae account when Blyth went on trial. He said that she had asked him ti dae it."

So Blyth had a reputation. Harry mused. This must be added to the file.

He left the group and made his way to the control in the annex.

The Inspector had gathered his team together and was reviewing all the evidence gathered so far.

"Let's begin with the events leading up to the discovery of the body in the ditch."

"The blacksmith lad, Donald McKay found the victim and reported it to P.C. Hamilton."

"So far, then, we have not been able to establish the identity of the girl."

"The length of time and the weather have not given much to go on when all traces may have been wiped out."

D.C. Penman observed, "Whoever put the body in the ditch must have been strong enough to handle such a weight. She was a healthy youngster and must have weighed about nine stone."

"Yes, point taken," the Inspector agreed. "We know from the post mortem report that she had been drinking wine immediately before she died. So, that indicates that she must have been in the company of someone who was accustomed to drinking wine. We are waiting on a report from the lab and it may be possible to tell what kind of wine she had been drinking."

"I can also say that marks on her ankles and wrists were doubtlessly caused by chains, and it was also evident that rings on her right hand had been removed as well as bracelets from her left arm."

"Who knows, we may find someone who can throw some light on the jewellery - where the chains came from?"

P.C. Dick Hamilton drew the Inspector's attention.

"I happen to be pretty well informed about the locals, and I have an idea that might be worth looking into."

The Inspector nodded. He was anxious to hear anything which could advance the investigations.

Hamilton continued, "It's the Laird. You see, although the man owns nearly everything you see around these parts, no one has seen him for some time."

"Is that unusual?" the Inspector was interested.

"Aye, we would have expected him to call in to ask about the finding o' the body. There's very little passes that man. He seems to ken aboot everything that goes on aboot the place."

"Have you any idea where the Laird may be at this time?"

"That's just the point Inspector, Naebody has a clue aboot the man."

P.C. Hamilton continued to outline most of the Laird's habits.

"He can usually be seen thrashing that poor mare across the fields and, of course, he calls in at the smithy to have the horse shod."

"He will, no doubt, visit the farm regularly?" added the Inspector.

"Well, as far as I ken, he leaves everything to Dave Anderson. Dave has managed the farm for years and makes a bloody good job o' it."

"Is there anything else you can tell us about this elusive Laird?"

"If he's no on his horse, he will be flashin' aboot in that swanky car."

"What kind of car is it?"

"It's a Talbot. My, but that's a braw motor. It's dark green and it has a lot o' shiny bits. Whit dae ye ca' that stuff?"

"Chromium?" D.C. Penman ventured to suggest.

"Aye, that's it. Chromium. The car has a lot of that stuff in the body. Oh, and there's anither thing. The tyres are white."

"A white, walled green Talbot with chromium trims," the Inspector mused. "That narrows the search quite a bit." "Thanks Dick, you've been very helpful."

Somehow, attention had been directed towards the landowner. Not so much on the man, but about his apparent absence from such a tragic occurrence in his estate. It was to be expected that the Laird would at least have shown some interest in the event in the village.

At this point in the discussion, Harry entered the control room and reported his encounter with the men at the well.

The revelation that, here, in their midst, Blyth was known as a man capable of rape came as a surprise and called for immediate consideration.

A talk with this Mr Blyth seemed to be next on the cards. The time factor made the estimate of the conditions existing when the body was placed in the ditch indefinite. Time and weather could have destroyed any clues around the vicinity and time was also a problem for the investigators when they were obliged to ask anyone to recollect their movements over a period of two months.

All possible measures were taken to preserve a record of likeness to the dead girl. It was obvious that her remains would decompose rapidly and it was imperative that such a record should be made.

The Inspector believed in discarding all the irrelevant details from their files by systematic elimination and it was apparent that the next step in the proceedings would have to be a visit to Mr Blyth.

Blyth lived with his father. Their home could be described as a hovel. Lacking the care and "the woman's touch', and reflecting a certain degree of laziness in the habits of the two men.

Blyth opened the door and his face expressed his obvious displeasure when he recognised the two men.

He offered no resistance to his visitors as he led the way to the living room.

His father was seated by the fire smoking a clay pipe and the evil smelling "thick-black tobacco'. The atmosphere in the house was unpleasant, the reason being that in addition to the heavy odour of the tobacco, there was the unmistakable smell of neglect in hygiene. The men's clothes and the general condition of the dwelling.

"We have called in for a routine chat," the Inspector began.

"We try to keep our records up-to-date."

Blyth shrugged, but said nothing in response.

"Can you tell us if you left the village at any time during the last two months?"

Blyth shook his head and sniggered. What a stupid question to be asked. Two months? How could anyone be expected to recall their movements over such a period of time.

"Are you asking me to tell you where I have been for the last twa months?" There was a hint of sarcasm in the question.

"No, not exactly, Mr Blyth."

Getting the man to talk was the Inspector's intention. There could be no progress with silence. What would be said and how it would be said would be carefully considered by the men trained in the art of interrogation.

The Inspector continued. "It is surprising how we can dig out the little things that happen to us when we try," he said.

"I've had dealings wi your kind before. You think ye are a' very clever."

"You have been questioned by the Police before?"

Blyth's father puffed that stinking clay pipe and said "Ye sill bugger." He sat at the fire shaking his head.

"Can you tell us why the Police were asking you questions?" Blyth knew instantly that he had slipped on a greasy patch. He knew immediately that his previous encounter with authority was related to his crime of rape some time ago. His mind began to race; a mental condition trained interrogators skilfully encouraged. This condition disturbed the trend of thought and produced confusion, which, in turn would certainly lead to the utterance of an unguarded word.

"I had nothing ti dae wi' that affair in the field," he said, relieved that he had found an answer which avoided any reference to the fact that he had served a prison sentence for rape.

The Inspector was aware that the unemployed travelled to town every week to collect their "dole' money.

"Have you been to town lately?"

Only on Thursday, that's when I collect my dole.

"So, that means, Mr Blyth, that you are in town every Thursday and is there any other day that you travel to town, say, to the pictures or to meet some friends?"

"Whit is this?" Ye are goin' on aboot asking me questions and ye are no sayin' why ye are askin'. Blyth was obviously being rattled by the Inspector's probing into his movements.

The Inspector made a note that he could easily check records at the Labour Exchange where it would be confirmed that the man had attended or had been absent on any particular day.

They had not made much progress, but the exercise had served to keep the man's name on the list of those who might provide a contribution to the list of missing date on the case in hand.

"I think that is all we need to talk about for the moment, Mr Blyth, and thank you for your time." The detectives made for the door. "Don't worry, we will see ourselves out."

As they walked, they reviewed the interview. Remarking on the man's manner and a certain evasions on particular points raised.

"Did you notice the state of his boots?", the D.C., asked.

"No, I missed that," confessed the Inspector.

"His boots were filthy, covered in what looked like garden soil. I wonder if he had been in his garden but then I noted that the garden at the house hadn't been cultivated apparently for years."

"Now that is a point worth a mention. Yes, we will keep that in mind."

CHAPTER EIGHT

Janet Farley was a friendly, young lady. It was a lovely day and she and her friends had decided to travel from Perth to spend the day in Dunfermline. Popular at school and ever ready with that smile.

Her parents adored their daughter and had high hopes for her academic future.

Vivacious and full of youthful fun, she excelled in sport and had developed a fine figure.

The warmth of the day had caused her to wear a light, summer dress, and she caught the eye of quite a few would be admirers.

It was her interest in photography, especially in capturing wild life and birds which led her into the path of the master of Craigmire Estate. The Laird was consumed with the recurrent urge to satisfy an unhealthy sexual impulse; lustful and cunning in the extreme to have avoided being associated in any way the disappearance of young girls who had recently come to the notice of Police all over the district.

Janet and her friends entered the Dunfermline Glen and began to enjoy the many attractions which were maintained in perfect order.

Her two friends had some errands to attend to and they all agreed that Janet could browse around the Glen until they returned. This suited the youngster because she had an idea that she was like to snap a peacock with its tail in full display.

She was seldom on her own when she left her home town, and had many friends. It so happened that, on that fateful day, her friends had left her to amuse herself with her camera.

After all, the Glen was a public place, where families enjoyed the open space and the recreation.

She walked along the pathways, humming to herself and swinging her sturdy No.2 Brownie by her side. Time to sit and rest and there, before her, was the bench occupied by a young couple and their two children.

There was space enough for her slim figure and she sat down to rest awhile.

Soon, the family left her on her own. A beautiful, young girl, with long hair flowing down her back, matching her delicate complexion.

Just the kind of target for a depraved observer, lurking and stalking in search of a potential victim.

She was soon too joined by a casual stranger, who showed no interest in her. At least, that is what she thought. Unseen, two evil eyes were pivoted nearly out of their sockets; drinking in every inch of her feminine form. Her face, her lips, her breasts; he lingered there for a while and then her shapely legs. The man's sensual appetite was stimulated by what he saw. He measured the girl from head to toe and over again, and she was quite unaware of his attention.

That ready smile. She smiled at the stranger and he appeared to notice her for the first time.

He nodded and put on his charm. His handsome appearance and deceptive sincerity would convince anyone that they were dealing with a perfectly normal gentleman.

He was a member of the "idle rich' class, and a menace to society.

It was easy to talk to this girl. She was so friendly, and what a coincidence, she shared his interest in cameras and birds.

"I see that you have a Kodak. They are quite good."

"It's all I can afford, but it will have to do until I can buy a better one."

"Yes, equipment is essential if we want to make a success of our hobby. I'm rather fortunate that I happen to have some of the tackle you are talking about."

Conversation was deliberately kept on a casual basis. At this delicate stage in their acquaintance, it was necessary to appear to be a stranger with no ulterior intention.

The girl was perfectly at east under the influence of the master of seduction.

The man was wise enough to know that it would be foolish to strike twice in the same area. A sequence would soon be the subject of investigation and that was the last thing he wanted to happen.

She looked at her black Brownie camera. It seemed so inadequate to the description he was now making of his superior "Roloflex', with its anastigmatic lens and all the other features attached to the expensive range of cameras.

"Some day, I might be able to afford a camera like that, she smiled. "In the meantime, my faithful little box here will have to do."

"Would you like to handle a good camera? I happen to have my old faithful in my car. It's parked just outside the park in the street."

Janet's enthusiasm blinded her to the risks involved with a stranger and foolishly agreed to follow him to the car.

They rose from the bench, chatting casually. The man impressed her with his indifference and charm and after all, it would be good to handle a really good camera. Such was the girl's craze for her hobby.

The success of his scheme lay in the attention he gave to planning the way ahead, together with his experience in luring the young and vulnerable to their ruin.

The green saloon, with its white walled tyres impressed the girl. This man must be very rich to be able to afford such a beautiful machine.

He reached into the car and produced a leather case from a glove box.

"Open it and have a look."

Her hands trembled as she fumbled with the spring catch on the case. The camera was indeed an expensive make and he pointed out the various features only such a camera could have incorporated in its design.

"Maybe, it is asking too much, but I see that you are very interested in photography and I happen to share your enthusiasm. Maybe you would like to use the camera. I have plenty of film."

"Could I?"

"Of course, my dear, but now, let me think, you don't want to snap the shops and the streets. Ah, I have it, I know a place where you can snap all the birds you ever dreamed of, they are at my place."

"Is it far from here?"

"No, not at all, only a few miles. I have an estate you see, and it's simply full of all kinds of birds. You will certainly enjoy being there."

Was this wise? Should she accept such an invitation from a complete stranger? He appeared to be a gentleman, and he had just mentioned his estate. She had no experience with the gentry. This might be quite an experience to see how the "other half' lived.

Today happened to be Martha's day off. She always left a tray for her master, in case he should return in her absence.

Janet was actually thrilled to be driven through the lodge gates, and along the drive to the huge mansion in the trees.

"Auntie will be pleased to see you. We seldom have visitors these days."

The reference to "Auntie' served to allay any reservations the girl may have had, and she happily followed the man through the massive front door and into the hall.

The tray with the food lay on a table where it would be convenient for the master to enjoy a snack.

"Auntie must be resting. We won't disturb her."

That accounted for the absence of "Auntie'.

She had never seen such luxury. The silver tray, covered with a white cloth. The pink marble stairway. She grimaced at the taste of the wine.

"Is the wine not to your liking? I am so sorry, won't be a tick."

Her host went off through a doorway and returned with another bottle of wine. "There now, how does that suit you?"

She ate a sandwich and drank some of the wine.

When she awoke, she couldn't understand.

Where was she? What kind of room was this? How did she get here?

Was that blood on the walls?

The sudden panic as she recovered partially from what had been the effects of a drug. She realised that she was lying on a large bed.

Chains? Yes, chains on her wrists and ankles. She was naked. Tugging the chains served only to make her wrists ache, and to convince her that she was unable to leave the bed.

She heard herself screaming. There was no-one to come to her assistance.

She screamed until her throat was dry, and she couldn't scream anymore.

The door opened and the man stood there before her. Naked. There are no words to describe the torment and mental anguish affecting the young girl.

The sight of the naked body. The aggressive attitude. His penis erect and throbbing in his excited state of anticipation.

He approached the bed slowly. Deliberately. Enjoying sadistically the frantic contortions of the body on the bed.

Nature was kind. Janet fainted.

She was unaware of the atrocity as the pervert satisfied his sexual lust on her body.

The luxury car drove away from the house and the body of young Janet Farley joined a skeleton in the family crypt.

Janet's two friends were exhausted. On their return to the park they had searched everywhere for their friend.

No-one had seen the young girl in a red dress carrying a camera.

A park-keeper, noticing their anxiety, asked if he could help them in any way. Unfortunately, he concluded that they had searched the entire area without success.

This was certainly a matter for the Police, and accordingly he led the two girls to his office and rang the local Police Station.

The girls assured the man that Janet would not have left the park when she had arranged to meet them at the Museum.

Wendy and Carol were in tears. Nothing like this had happened before. All kinds of thoughts passed through their minds. The doubt. The uncertainty. The waiting. In a strange town they felt vulnerable and afraid. This was an entirely new experience for them as they waited for the arrival of the Police.

Within ten minutes of the call, two Policemen arrived and began to question the two girls. The park-keeper provided most of the relevant information and after they were satisfied that they had recorded all the details available at that time, the Police suggested that the girls should return to their home in Perth.

Wendy and Carol reluctantly agreed. They knew that they could not assist the Police any further.

The Police escorted them to the "bus station and made sure that they boarded the correct bus.

The journey back to Perth seemed to be so much longer than usual. They talked about their feelings of hopelessness and frustration. The speculation and the dreadful possibilities they dare not think about.

Their immediate concern on arrival was to visit Janet's parents. In some way, they felt partly responsible for the fact that they had not been able to locate their friend, but like many others, they had been affected by that common believe that "It can never happen to us.'

Janet's parents were alarmed at the news that the excited girls had to tell, and without hesitation, they prepared to travel to Dunfermline.

They were blissfully unaware that, as they travelled, Janet, their daughter was passing through the hellish torment, pain and terror, chained on a bed in the mansion of Craigmire.

Janet's father attempted to console his wife by telling her what she already knew. There was bound to be an explanation. Janet can't have vanished. There must be some trace of her whereabouts and the Police were bound to find the clues to her disappearance.

It was about six o'clock when they arrived at the Police station when they were told that no progress had been made in the search for their daughter.

In desperation, they walked through the streets in the vain hope that per chance they would find some sign which would lead them to the girl with the ready smile.

Janet's father reflected on the many previous occasions when he had read news about someone disappearing and how he had simply turned the page to read about something else.

This was no item of news to be read and passed over lightly. It was reality. The fact was beginning to assert itself. Reality; Janet, their loved one was the subject of attention. The uncertainty and the dread had come to them with all the tragic possibilities.

Whilst the perpetrator gloated over his prize, the victims suffered the agony and despair and the loss.

CHAPTER NINE

Another hard day's work in the book shop in town and Monica, having spent the evening with Donald at his home, was ready to a good night's sleep.

She laid back the sheets on her bed and sat down before the dressing table mirror, where she brushed her hair.

A dark shadow moved stealthily in the garden below her bedroom window. Quietly, he raised a ladder and rested it against the window sill.

The bedroom air was stifling and Monica had opened it wide.

The man climbed steadily, making no sound and stopped when he had a perfect view of the bedroom.

His depraved mind willed the girl to undress. To expose her body. He saw no evil in what he was doing. This was a free strip show. He was content to watch in silence and to enjoy this intrusion into a young girl's privacy.

Monica put on her night gown and popped into bed. It was then "lights out'.

The intruder descended and replaced the ladder against the fence where it was suspended on hooks to preserve it.

Monica went to sleep, completely unaware that she had been the object of the eyes of a sexual pervert.

The shadowy figure faded into the dark and was gone.

Mrs Anderson wasn't a keen gardener, but she had one hobby which the family enjoyed when she enhanced the family meal with the flavour of her specially grown herbs.

Her Herb garden was situated directly below Monica's bedroom window, and it was her habit to visit the garden every morning.

The marks in the garden soil attracted her attention. She knew that she had not made the impression, and closer examination led her to the conclusion that the marks had been made with the strings of a ladder.

Yes, there was a ladder hanging on the fence and that could have been the ladder used. But why? Who would have been using the ladder at that particular position? She went over to the ladder and there was soil on the base of the strings. The soil was fresh and she knew that in the heat of summer, earth can dry quickly.

Dave should be told about this, she decided. Already, there was a growing feeling of concern in her mind. To her knowledge, no one had been told to do anything which would require the use of a ladder against the farm house.

David Anderson was suspicious immediately he saw the imprints of the ladder. Looking up, he became alarmed. "My god, that's Monica's bedroom and look, see the marks on the wall below the window sill. Someone has been using a ladder to reach Monica's window."

Dave and his wife went into the farmhouse and talked about this problem. It was serious when their daughter's bedroom was evidently the target.

Monica was awake, as usual, she slept soundly and had no difficulty in opening her eyes to welcome another day.

Dressed, she went downstairs and had breakfast with her parents, completely unaware that she had been the object of a peep show the previous evening.

Her father was very concerned about her safety. There were too many "ifs' about these days. Too many possibilities.

Would the murderer strike again? and where would he carry out his criminal practice.

Together, he and his wife told their daughter about the events which had taken place in the morning. The ladder and her open window. Monica was embarrassed and slightly shocked at the thought of being watched whilst she was preparing to go to bed.

"Don't worry, my dear, he'll be caught. I'll grant you that." Dave felt renewed anger boiling up inside.

It is one thing reading about such experiences happening to others but when the hand of fate turns towards us everything is entirely different.

We learn to feel the anger and the grief and the pain of the uncertainty of what may have occurred to us.

He made sure that his daughter would be escorted to the "bus on her way to town and to work.

Donald had already appointed himself her escort when she was on her way home.

In fact, the entire village was on the alert and taking no chances with the young ones. A village held in the grip of fear.

Dave knew the men who worked for him and he was certain that none of them could be implicated in this latest episode.

Whoever did this perverted act was someone other than the workers on the farm. He did not rule out some of the residents in the village.

There were several characters who might fit the description of a person capable of climbing a ladder to watch a young girl in her bedroom and apart from the investigation into the tragic murder of the girl in the ditch, it was obviously a matter of elimination of all who could be described as suspects.

Dave decided to inform the Police about this. They would know how best to deal with the matter.

Jennie Liddel took his call and connected him to the Police department.

Dave had a suspicion that Jennie would treat anything she heard as a sensation and spread it around. On this occasion, he was glad that he had remembered Jennie's weakness and warned her not to talk about what she might hear regarding this telephone call.

Inspector Gilmour was ordered to investigate this mystery and it was emphasised that, in view of all the other incidents which had come to light during the past few weeks, nothing should be allowed to pass without attention.

The information he had to start with was not conclusive, although the report that a ladder had been used against the wall without authority suggested the possibility that there had been an attempt to make an entry.

Dave met the Inspector and D.C. Penman and took them to the side of the farmhouse, where the ladder had been used.

The imprints on the soil matched the space between the strings of the ladder hanging on the fence and the marks on the wall were also significant.

"It definitely appears to be a case of attempted entry, or, I hesitate to say this," the Inspector looked at Dave and he could see the idea flooding into the farmer's expression.

"He wizna' attemptin' to go in. He wiz just lookin?" The Inspector nodded. "A peeping Tom."

D.C. Penman reminded the Inspector about the soil on Blyth's boots. Garden soil? and the man had not been working in his own garden? "You may have a point here and it is worth looking into."

Dave was furious. He began to work out in his mind all the possibilities where his daughter could have been the reason for the interest of a peeping tom. The mention of Blyth brought to mind the unpopular brute in the village with his broken nose and sullen expression. Monica's father also recalled the case against the man when he was sentenced to imprisonment for rape.

"If it turns out to be that bastard, he is no' jist a peepin' tom - he's a rapist."

"Yes, we know about Blyth's record, Mr Anderson, but we cannot jump to conclusions; at least for the moment. We will, of course, have a chat with that man as soon as we can."

Then Dave's sharp eye saw the imprint on the garden soil. The mark of a boot.

"Look", he said, pointing, "is that the mark o' a boot?"

"It certainly is, and it is recent as you will see. The earth hasn't had time to dry out. It's still fresh. It must have been made last night."

D.C. Penman was ahead of his superior.

"Plaster cast?"

"As soon as you can, organise it John, and meanwhile," he looked at Dave. "We must make sure that this is not disturbed. I'll send a man up as soon as I can."

"Ye can use the "phone, but I have to warn ye, that Jennie Liddel is a gossip and if she gets wind o' what is going on here, she'll have it a' o'er the place."

"Yes, good thinking, Dave." "Now if I can use your "phone?"

Without making any definite reference to what was required, the Inspector managed to direct P.C. Hamilton to join them at the farm.

Dave volunteered to keep an eye on the garden and this allowed the two men to leave and make their way to call on Blyth, which seemed to be the most urgent business at present.

Already, the Inspector was mulling over the case which might be established to confirm guilt.

He had the imprint in the garden soil, and the soil on Blyth's boots.

The man's record was secondary.

It was about nine o'clock in the morning and the Blyth's had no particular reason to rise early and to enjoy the benefits of the summer's day. They were in bed.

D.C. Penman's loud, authoritative knock on their door aroused the two from their slumbers, and Blyth eventually appeared at the door in his shirt. He obviously didn't use pyjamas.

"Whit the hell?"

"Good morning, Mr Blyth, we want another word with you. Can we come in?"

Entering that stinking hovel, especially in the morning when the two men had just awakened from a sleep was quite an ordeal.

A barefooted Blyth led the way indoors.

D.C. Penman made directly for the man's boots.

"He, whit are ye doin' wi' my boots?"

"We are just having a look at the soil on your boots, Mr Blyth."

"Kin a man no' hae dirty boots, without the Polis wantin' tae see them?"

"Have you another pair of boots, Mr Blyth?"

"Are ye kiddin', hoo kin a man on the dole have twa pair o' boots, dinna be daft."

The Inspector recalled the arrival of the mail that morning and he had a large brown envelope in his pocket. He gave this to D.C. Penman, who scraped the soil from the boots into the envelope.

"Where were you last night, Mr Blyth?"

The question took the man by surprise.

Guilt and the presence of two experienced Police officials was unnerving. Fear was quite apparent. The man was obviously attempting to conceal guilt with an exaggerated sequence of facial expressions. Threatening, submission, amused, confused.

He knew that he had to think quickly and that was not one of his strong points.

"I wiz in the hoose," he answered.

"All during the evening and during the night?"

"Aye, a' the time."

"And you didn't leave the house at any time?"

"Have you worked on the farm or in the fields?"

"Me, naw, I'm on the dole. Ye canny work when ye're on the dole."

"I'm not trying to trick you about the dole, Mr Blyth, I simply want to know if you are acquainted with the farm and the fields around."

"I've lived here a' ma life. I should ken my way aboot the place."

"We have to make absolutely sure about all the little details we come across. For instance, you wouldn't happen to have seen any strangers in the area lately?"

Blyth hesitated. His face was transparent. Thoughts rushing through his mind caused his expression to change. He was absorbed in an attempt to appear to be calm.

There are many and varied opinions on the subject of crime and offences in general.

Motivation being the most popular area of consideration in the conclusion of the question. Why? With intent>

There are those who contend that genetic inheritance is mainly the cause attributed to the commission of crime. The criminal is weak and has no will to resist the temptation placed in his way.

Blyth certainly was the victim of circumstances beyond his control. His parents had learned at an early age that their son could present a problem to society. Disobedient, aggressive and sadly lacking in intelligence.

Blyth had learned early in life his incapacity to match the performance of others and consequently relied increasingly on his physical strength to seek the dominance he craved. He would settle an argument with his fists.

The Inspector began to assess the course he was following and it became increasingly clear to him that there was not sufficient evidence to accuse this man with the offence of "Peeping Tom.'

Gradually, he guided the course of the interview away from the farm and introduced a substitute reason for their enquiry.

"Well now Mr Blyth, you have satisfied us that you have nothing more to add to our enquiries, and I know that you will agreed that our work has to be thorough and I'm sorry is we have inconvenienced you and your father this morning."

The sudden change and release from pressure showed clearly on Blyth's expression. Confidence returned to his voice and even went as far as to sympathise with the two men.

"Oh forget it, we a' ken you lads have a job to dae."

The two men left the Blyth home, once again savouring the thrust of clean, country air into their lungs, which was such a contrast to the unhealthy atmosphere within these dark walls, where the simple-minded man grinned his relief in the mistaken belief that the Police had eliminated him from their enquiries.

When they were out of sight of the Blyth house, the Inspector began to explain why he had terminated the enquiry.

"We simply don't have enough to go on to convict the man, and I'm beginning to hatch an idea how we might net the bounder."

"Watch him?", the D.C. enquired.

"Not exactly, let's get back to control and we can talk over my idea over a cup of tea."

D.C. Penman's mind turned to Donald. He gasped.

"Well, what's the matter, John?"

"It has just occurred to me that Donald McKay will go off like a rocket when he finds out about the peeping Tom."

"My goodness, John, you're right. We must do something about that right away."

They both changed their direction and made for the Smithy.

Donald was hammering a red hot iron on his anvil when they walked into the blacksmith's shop.

"Hello Donald, when you're finished, can we have a word with you?"

The Inspector tried to be as casual as possible under the circumstances. Donald laid his tools on the forge and followed the two men outside.

"Whit is it, have ye made any progress?"

"No, Donald, it is nothing to do with the body you found, something else has turned up and we think we should have a talk about it."

Donald peered at the two men with some interest.

"Before you hear what I have to say, Donald, I want you to listen and I want you to stay calm, just listen and don't fly off the handle."

He gave the lad time to take all this in and smiled reassuringly. He knew that he was treading on delicate ground.

They both had a growing feeling that it would be necessary to pounce on the lad and hold him down, once he had been told that his pretty young sweetheart had been the object of a peeping Tom.

Their instincts were right of course, the young "smith' had to be grabbed and forcibly held until he calmed down.

A peeping Tom at the farm? His girlfriend! Donald's thoughts raged out of control for a moment.

The Inspector gave the lad all the details and went as far as to tell him about a plan he had thought out to find the culprit.

Donald was eager to offer his assistance, but there was a certainty that there would be no controlling the boy should the pervert be found.

"It's like this Donald, we don't want to give anyone the idea that we're working on this matter. We want to appear as normal as possible, so when you go back to work, just make up a story; anything; as long as it isn't anything to do with what we have been talking about."

Donald understood the importance of what the Inspector was saying and nodded. He found it difficult to contain his anger. He knew that there was nothing he could do to find the beast who had gloated over the scene in Monica's bedroom. He felt so frustrated, so inadequate, so angry.

Bracing himself, he returned to the forge and explained to his workmates that the Police were anxious to recall every detail about his gruesome find in the ditch.

CHAPTER TEN

During the 1930's, the Co-operative movement accounted for a large share of the retail trade and manufacturing "Co-op' products for sale.

Membership of the "Society' entitled customers to accumulate a "Dividend' accrued from the profits.

The payment of the quarterly "Divvy' marked the occasion when the family could go to town on a spending spree (mostly in co-operative retail shops).

When need arose anywhere within the area, a co-operative branch would be opened. Staffed by local people, these branches provided work for the young and old. The young, benefiting from the experience and graduating to senior positions as they were upgraded.

Co-operative vans were a familiar sight in the town and villages; the butchers, the baker and many other facilities and services were known throughout the land.

Craigmire had its fair share in the attentions and provisions of the Co-operative Society and as the distribution vans arrived, they provided an opportunity for the local residents to meet and have a chat and an exchange of views and news.

At the rear of the baker's van, the "baker man' was well known to the women of the village. He was expected to share a joke and to create a great deal of hilarity with all his experienced routine and banter.

Jock Turner was always his usual, jocular, breezy self and a popular employee of the "Co-op'. He was also the bearer of news and it is possible that this feature of the man's sales' ability was more of an attraction than his bread and buns.

When he opened the doors of the can, the assembled group would savour the wholesome aroma of warm bread; the staple diet of the working class.

Jockie grinned at the women assembled around him with the bread baskets. "Any mair bodies been found in the village?"

Aggie Wishart was first in the queue. "Ye have an awfa' nerve, Jockie, whit a thing to say."

"I'm hearing a' sorts of stories aboot Craigmire, and it is sometimes difficult to believe whit ye read in the papers."

The women nodded unanimously with the breadman.

"It's a tragedy, right enough. That poor lassie cut doon in her prime" commented Mrs Brown, "and the Polis dinna seem ti be any further forwards."

Jockie sounded confident. "They'll catch the blighter, jist you wait and see."

"I widna like their job" Aggie had always something to say.

Jock had a talent for selling bread. He could leave a group of women grasping a pile of loafs, unaware that they had bought them.

He was also the local courier and could be relied upon to convey details of the latest scandal as well as all the "hatches', "matches' and "despatches'.

"By the way, that lassie they found could be the youngster who went missin' in Dunfermline aboot two months ago."

He moved away, leaving in his wake that rich aroma of wholesome bread. The women returned to their homes with baskets laden with another supply of the "staple diet'.

Lizzie Duncan had heard the reference to the missing girl and wondered if, by chance, the Police were aware of her disappearance. She decided to clear her mind on the matter and to have a word with the Inspector.

The opportunity presented itself sooner than she had expected. The two officers were on their way to the control after having talked to Blyth.

"Hello Inspector, can I have a word wi' ye?"

"Why yes of course, Mrs Duncan I believe?" We might as well step inside the shop. It might stop a lot of crazy rumours going about."

Lizzie led the way to the rear of the shop and related the information she had heard from Jockie the Baker.

Reg was immediately alert. This is what he had hoped for, a missing girl and two months ago. That would fit in well with the time of death estimated by the coroner.

"It's maybe nothing ti dae wi' that poor lass they found in the ditch, but I thocht it wiz best ti tell ye aboot it."

"You did the right thing, Mrs Duncan and to tell you the truth, I am grateful to you for taking the trouble."

Somehow, he had the feeling that he had the first real contact with the trail of facts that would eventually be uncovered.

This matter must receive immediate attention. Headquarters would be asked to trace the list of missing persons and it would be an advantage to them to have a date associated with their search through the files.

The Police had no computers during the 1930's. Records were kept in writing on paper and filed for reference in an indexed card system.

Meanwhile, after he had signalled his request to headquarters, the Inspector began to unravel all the evidence against Blyth. It was essential that more conclusive evidence should be unearthed to secure a conviction.

Then the idea occurred to him that the man with the broken nose could be tricked into making a mistake.

Acting on the assumption that Blyth would not be satisfied with one visit to the farmhouse, the obvious procedure would be to prepare a situation where the suspect would be caught in the act.

He discussed the idea with his staff and they agreed that there was a possibility that a plan could be devised which would produce the desired result. The capture of a man who was a menace to society.

Accompanied by Dick Hamilton and D.C. Penman, the Inspector returned to the farm.

The arrangements were simple. The bedroom window would be opened and the scene set to lure the pervert into a position where he could be said to have committed an offence. There was no question of "entrapment'.

The timing was crucial. When would the man return to the farmhouse? Had the fact that he had been questioned deter the man and most importantly, Monica would have to be brought into the plot to play her part.

As far as the girl was concerned, to ensure her safety, she would not be involved directly with the affair. It was agreed that she should sleep elsewhere until the man had been caught.

Summing the character of Blyth, the Inspector was confident that, provided he had not been scared off, he would not be satisfied with one "peep' into the girl's bedroom.

D.C. Hardy was the smallest of the three men and he was chosen to be the bait. He would occupy Monica's bed and the two officers would be in a position to take the necessary action when the time arrived.

Blyth would be kept under observation and it was Hendry Ashford's house which provided the observation post. The house was ideally situated to maintain a round-the-clock watch on the Blyth home.

Ashford readily agreed to co-operate with the Police in this operation. The man could be trusted to render assistance without any difficulties arising from his involvement. It was also evident that Ashford had no regard to the aggressive pervert who had been involved in many questionable incidents in the past.

The Police had most of the daytime to work on other matters as there would certainly be no movement of the suspect before sundown.

The Inspector reflected on the events of the morning. He felt that, with the responsibility of the murder investigation, he had enough to deal with.

There was always the possibility that the wayward Mr Blyth could have been involved in the death of the girl in the ditch.

He had demonstrated, beyond doubt, that he was capable of molesting and attacking young girls, and this latest incident, where it was assumed that he had been the peeping Tom at the farmhouse, increased the justification for placing him on the list of suspects.

Now the Inspector had a new development to deal with, which seemed to be promising. The report, however vague, that a girl had been missing from home required some explanation. If she could not be traced, her family could assist in the identification of the girl found in the ditch. It would amount to a positive result, or the elimination of another event concerning missing persons.

Jockie Turner, the bread man, didn't know it, but he had some explaining to do.

The C.I.D., officers in Dunfermline met the man before he left on his daily rounds and questioned him about the story he had told about the missing girl.

The officers were led to an address in Milesmark in Dunfermline, where they met the parents of Margaret Wilson, who had apparently responded to an advert in the local newspaper concerning a vacancy for a domestic servant.

According to her parents, Margaret had left home and had, as far as they believed, been successful in her quest for work.

Her parents were awaiting a letter from their daughter, reporting how she was established in a secure post.

Mrs Wilson's attitude changed dramatically when she was faced with the Police enquiries regarding her daughter's movements about two months ago. She admitted that she was beginning to feel worried about the delay since Margaret had left home, but explained that this was not altogether unusual. Margaret was not one to keep her affairs up-to-date.

It was with great difficulty that the officers persuaded Mrs Wilson to accompany them to the Police Station where the photographs of the girl found in the ditch at Craigmire could be seen.

This was all a matter of routine for the men who dealt with crime and all its variations, but to an anxious mother the experience was devasting. The uncertainty. The hope that what she would be given to look at would not be her daughter.

The officers knew what must have been going on in their passenger's mind and tried to make the conversation a focus on diversionary matters. They were aware that their kindly attempts were meaningless to the distraught mother seated in the Police car, subconsciously clasping her hands, staring ahead with unseeing eyes.

The Police photographers had made a reasonable likeness of the dead girl, which was no mean task.

The photograph was to essentially represent as near a likeness to the subject as possible. The fact that the body was rigid when it was discovered made the task complicated and called for the expertise required to portray life in a subject who wore the mask of death.

The Inspector, Murray, asked Mrs Wilson to have a seat whilst he explained the discovery of a girl in Craigmire, and how the Police were required to establish her identity.

"We are not, at this stage, suggesting that the evidence we are about to show you has any connection with your daughter, but it will assist us greatly, Mrs Wilson, if you would take a look at these photographs and tell us if you recognise any of them.

Gently, he offered the woman one of the photographs and her reaction was immediate. She screamed. She had recognised her daughter, Margaret, despite the effect of lifelessness, it was her daughter.

Inspector Murray called a Policewoman to counsel the mother and nodded to his colleagues. They left the room.

Confirmation of the identity of the dead girl was rushed to Inspector Gilmour.

This was indeed a positive step forward. It was now a matter of recounting the movements of the dead girl and to find, if possible, the advertisement she had noticed in the local newspaper.

The name of the person advertising would be a point in the right direction.

The Coroner's inquest into the death of the girl had placed the legal obligation to find the killer on investigation. The killing had been committed by "Person, or persons unknown.' Naming the person was one thing. The provision of evidence to secure a conviction was another.

There are so many so-called loopholes in the law. Training and experience in the gathering of such information. Definition and presentation of the facts. Questioning and all the rules attendant upon that activity had to be conducted in such a manner as to prevent any likelihood of failure to prosecute the offender.

Authorisation was granted for the burial of the dead girl and the family made arrangements accordingly.

The effect on relatives of a murdered person cannot be described in words. A death due to natural causes or by accident has no relationship with the unknown speculation associated with the unlawful taking of life.

The family were devastated. How had their daughter died? Where had she died? Who had killed her? These were some of the questions mingling with the torment in their hearts and minds as they paid their final respect to the one they loved.

The funeral attracted a great deal of attention from the press and the public. The press were motivated purely on commercial grounds, whilst the members of the public who stood in silence around the grave could be classified as the sympathetic and those who were there possessed with that morbid curiosity which singles out the people who have little else to do and who revel in sensationalism and idle gossip.

The publicity created by the funeral and the mention of the village of Craigmire sparked off further developments in the process of the investigation.

When Hazel Murray's aunt and uncle read the news in St. Andrews, they became anxious. They had expected their niece to arrive to stay with them three days ago and had written to the girl's parents in York asking for information. Had Hazel left home to journey to St. Andrews? If so, when had she left?"

This sensational event, so near to their home, gave them just cause for alarm.

They didn't hesitate. The possibilities were only too clear now that it was realised that their niece would have been in the vicinity of Craigmire on her way to St. Andrews.

The local Police were very thorough; recording every word in writing as the anxious couple reported their problem.

This was not a report of a missing person, but, in the light of publicity given to the latest outrage - the murder of a teenage girl, it was considered appropriate to circulate any reference to persons missing to neighbouring authorities.

Inspector Gilmour's attention was drawn to the message from St. Andrews and considering the number of questions yet to be answered, it was necessary that the information should be included in the growing file on the Craigmire mystery.

CHAPTER ELEVEN

A week had passed since the body had been found in the ditch and the Police had little to go on apart from the identity of the victim.

The fact that the body had been found in one particular area seemed at first glance to suggest that the person or persons responsible were located somewhere in the vicinity.

The fact that the Laird had not been seen in the area did not escape Inspector Gilmour's attention. He had notified his superiors that finding the Honourable James Harper-Nelson was a matter or priority. It was known, however, that the landowner had frequently to travel south to London to attend to some of his financial affairs.

Efforts were being made to trace the man.

Indeed, the Honourable James Harper-Nelson lived in space.

Whilst the authorities were searching for him he was standing in Waverly Station.

He had no close friends and little was known about the man who owned Craigmire estate.

He spent a great deal of his time in Edinburgh, where he was known as a silent man, who frequented various "water holes' in the city.

The fact that he regularly visited the Waverly Station had escaped the notice of the authorities. This behaviour would seem odd under any circumstances, when it was associated with a man of the Laird's social status.

The well dressed gentleman had a dual personality.

Standing alone, he was intent on simply watching. Waiting, day after day. Watching everyone who passed by on their way out of the station.

He knew exactly what he was looking for. He was intent on finding a young girl on her own. In a mind warped with an unhealthy lust, he could not resist the overpowering demands an inner voice dictated to him.

To make contact with a desirable female totally absorbed him.

This was not a new adventure. He had patrolled this action-packed pitch several times with success. The thought struck him and he smiled inwardly. All this time and no one had any idea that the Hon. J. Harper-Nelson was responsible for the disappearance of several young girls.

Hazel Murray was eighteen years of age. She had just arrived in Edinburgh on the "Flying Scotsman' from London.

The green monster stood in the terminus, panting and hissing in clouds of steam and vibrating with the heat and unspent power.

The girl emerged through the white shroud with the other passengers thrusting their way in all directions.

Fate would have it that, at that instant, she stood alone and was thus conspicuous. Easily seen. Singled out to anyone looking for one such as she.

The Laird saw her. He saw the two large suitcases. They appeared to be heavy.

Everything he had wished for fell into place. Here was the young, attractive girl, alone? Yes. Alone. His perverted mind collected all the details and calculated their merits.

Obviously she was a stranger, as she looked anxiously around the profusion of signs and directions.

The predator watched his prey, his agile mind appraising the situation. Were people watching her progress? Was anyone in the crowd showing the slightest interest in her?

He moved into a position which he judged would cross her path. She moved closer. "Can I help you, young lady?"

He was charming. She felt no sense of unease.

"I'm lookin' for the train for Fife," she said.

"Can you please direct me to the right platform?"

"Now, that is a coincidence, I happen to be on my way there too. Perhaps I can help you with your luggage. It seems to be very heavy for a pretty young lady like you."

What a kind, helpful gentleman, she thought. He looked every part the gentleman. His tweed suit and brown boots. Yes, she concluded, this man was a member of the gentle class.

"Yes, thank you, you are very kind."

"It will be a pleasure, I'm sure." He took her luggage and led the way to platform 27.

The Fife train was waiting.

"I travel First," he explained. "You will be Third?"

"Yes, I am afraid that you are right. I am a Third class passenger, and now we must part company."

Unseen the Laird had slipped a pound note into the porter's hand.

"Look, there's no need for you to travel Third. You can be my guest. Come, and you can sample the luxury of First Class travel."

He led the way to the First Class carriage. He was carrying her luggage and it somehow hadn't occurred to her that she was having little opportunity to choose what she should do.

103

No matter, this was indeed a public place and she had no sense of danger. On the contrary. She found herself relating to this stranger with all the veneer of the well-to-do.

After they had been seated in the comparative comfort of the luxurious carriage, he proceeded with a deliberate strategy of finding out all he could.

Hazel co-operated innocently. She was on her way to St. Andrews to live with her aunt and to attend the University.

This was perfect. He could see his way forward now.

"St. Andrews is quite a journey from Dunfermline. You will need to take a "bus."

"I see, and just how far away is St. Andrews?"

"It's some forty miles, I would say."

"Oh, I had no idea it would be so far away."

"Don't worry, my dear, I will be able to direct you to the "bus station when we reach Dunfermline."

The girl settled herself into the deep upholstery and felt completely relaxed.

She was also completely unaware of two eyes measuring and literally feeding on her sexuality. Her breasts, her lips, her hair, her shapely legs. The eyes appraised her attributes over and over again.

He was being stimulated and it was with great difficulty that he concealed his perceptions from her.

They had lapsed into silence and Hazel began to reflect on her journey from London.

Things couldn't have worked out better. A First Class carriage and a charming gentleman as a guide in a strange land.

He pointed out interesting features on the way. The Forth Bridge and hills visible in the north.

Rosyth, Inverkeithing.

"We won't be long now," he said and reached to the luggage rack to bring down her luggage.

Dunfermline Lower Station and through the barrier.

Taxis were waiting in line.

She stood looking around her.

He smiled and pointed to a dark, green Talbot saloon, heavily embellished with chromium trims.

"Is that your car?" she asked, amazed.

"Yes, indeed, I always park it there when I am in Edinburgh. It is handy and saves a lot of footwork. I say! maybe it is presumptuous of me, but can I offer you a lift to the "bus station if you care to accept the offer of a stranger?"

That was his first mistake. He knew immediately that he should have avoided any reference to the relationship. His mind raced to find the antidote to the first sign of alarm. Had he lost this one?

To his great relief, she asked if the "bus station was far from the railway station.

That charming smile again. It gave her reassurance. It set her mind at rest. He explained that the "buses were not too far away.

Then a brilliant diversion!

"You must be starving, when did you last eat?"

She had been so involved with all that had happened in the last hour that she was unaware that she was, in fact, quite hungry.

"It will be two hours before you reach your destination and you might as well stop off for a quick snack."

He was quite right, of course and his follow-up clinched the matter. "I could do with a snack myself."

Driving on northwards in the wrong direction. "I know just the place," he said.

He was such a charmer that his intended victim failed to observe that they had left the town and were in open countryside.

He turned the car into the driveway at Craigmire and reassured her that this detour would not delay her boarding the "bus in town.

"My aunt will be pleased to see you, my dear. We can have tea at my place."

"Is this your place?" she asked in amazement.

"Yes, indeed, my family have had this estate for generations." He was so capable of finding the right words on such occasions.

The mansion was partially visible in the fading light. Hazel did not see the dereliction and decay. She saw a very large mansion house, albeit in the gloom and this impressed her.

She was slightly concerned about how she would behave in the presence of the aunt, her companion had mentioned.

"Leave your luggage in the car. We won't be long here," he said.

Martha appeared. She stood obediently in silence. Waiting for orders from her master.

"Ah, there you are, Martha. Can you rustle up a pot of tea and some of your famous sandwiches?"

It was all so acceptable. So natural. So kind.

There followed a lengthy exposition of the family history and of course, that non-existent aunt.

"Auntie must be resting." That would settle any apprehension for a while.

The efficient housekeeper arrived with tea and all the essentials and swept out of sight, closing the door quietly.

Hazel poured the tea and was grateful for the chance to have something to eat.

She was, of course, completely unaware that the nasty man, with all his charm, had slipped something into her tea.

Acting quickly, the Laird lifted the girl onto his shoulder and mounted the pink marble stairway.

He passed the living quarters which were in daily use and unlocked a door.

Descending the stairs, he called to Martha and told her that the girl had gone.

There was a message on Inspector Gilmour's desk. He was required to call at the hospital in Dunfermline, and to contact a patient in ward six.

Campbell was a sorry sight. Strapped in bed with plaster on one leg and an arm in a sling.

"What happened to you?" was the obvious question.

"Two or three days ago, I was driving back to town when this madman came out of a side road and sent me head on into a tree."

"There are not so many vehicles on the roads these days, you are bound to have taken a note of what kind of car was involved. Anyway, how are you feeling now?"

"I feel as if I had whacked a tree," Campbell grinned.

"You wanted to speak to me?"

"Yes, I'm sorry about the delay in getting in touch with you, but as you see," Campbell swept his hand over the plastered leg, "I have been out for the count until this morning."

"You must have had quite a wallop."

"I was in a bit of a hurry too."

"This crazy guy? What kind of car would you say he was driving?"

"It was real swank, dark green with white walled tyres."

The Inspector's mind began to work on the possibility that the Laird had returned to the estate. Only such as he could afford the luxury of such a car.

Campbell was anxious to give the Inspector the details of his visit to the estate.

"I visited the manor house before I got this." He indicated to his plastered leg. "There was no reply to my banging on the door and no-one appeared to be about, so I had to abandon the idea of having a word with the Laird. Before I left that awful place, I took a snapshot of the house. You never know when you will need to use these random photos. I had walked to the house because my car was in the village and the rest of the pack were watching me. If I had taken my car they would have crowded me out before I got to the house. That is why I was walking back up the drive to the lodge and I noticed that the family crypt had been disturbed. That's a queer place. Makes you feel the goose pimples creeping up your back. The iron gate was partly open and it had obviously been moved quite recently, judging by the state of the weeds. Someone has obviously gone into the place as there were broken twigs on the shrubs. Inside, there are lots of stone coffins and one had a lid that had been moved aside and had not been replaced. There was a skeleton inside, and it had two rings on a finger."

The Inspector was engrossed in the tale which Campbell was excitedly telling. "Which finger and which hand?"

Campbell thought for a moment and nodded, as if in agreement with the decision he had reached, "Yes, the rings were on the third finger of the left hand."

"A woman most likely," the Inspector observed.

"There was another body in that tomb."

"Not another young girl?"

"Yes, indeed, there is no mistake, she was naked and had obviously been thrown in on top of the skeleton. I grabbed my car and decided to report directly to you and this is where I ended up." Campbell gestured despairingly and continued. "The photograph I took; he indicated to his locker by the bedside; I took that before I left the big house."

The Inspector reached into the locker and brought out a folder. The pictures were of the big house and McKenzie, the gamekeeper.

"Look at the windows."

Reg rearranged the photo of the house and looked enquiringly at Campbell.

"Do you see a face at the window?"

Reg saw it immediately now that it was drawn to his attention. There was definitely the image of a face at an upstairs window and the bars. The large window was barred.

"Campbell, you've hit the jackpot, old man. Don't worry about the delay, you couldn't help being admitted to hospital.

The Inspector showed signs of restlessness and Campbell smiled.

"Go on Inspector, I know that you're desperate to get going on that information, don't let a dying may stop you."

Reg patted the plastered leg gently as a gesture of his appreciation and left the newsman.

His mind was churning over the startling revelations he had just received and somehow he felt his mind concentrating on the estate. McKenzie? He had met the dour Scot with his shotgun and his instincts caused him to reject the idea that the gamekeeper was a pervert and one capable of committing the murders.

The Laird? This was different. He hadn't met the Laird of Craigmire and it now seemed imperative that this should be remedied as soon as possible.

First, he must return to the village and organise a party of men who would accompany him to the estate. Before this though, he must talk to Hendry Ashford.

The Inspector did not relish this next assignment.

Hendry Ashford had to be faced with the ordeal of confirming the identity of the rings found on the skeleton in the crypt.

On his way to the cottage he went over in his mind the way in which he would introduce the vital question. Did Hendry Ashford recognise the rings?

There was no way of knowing how the man would react. Reg was aware that the man had suffered a grievous loss a few days after he and his wife had settled in their cottage, looking ahead to a life of love and marriage.

He knew that the couple had spent their life savings on furnishings, their prospects terminated abruptly and without explanation. The young bride had vanished.

Lizzie Duncan had described the tragic days which had followed the day the young bride had disappeared.

The activities of Police, the questions, the suspicions and the searching in every possible location where a body might have been concealed.

The Inspector was to receive the answer to these questions from a totally unexpected source.

Meanwhile, he found himself knocking on the door. Hendry was a friendly man, he earned a living of sorts painting landscapes and other subjects and had exceptional talent in carving wood. Searching the woodlands for parts of trees which, by their natural shape in growth, suggested a form only the discerning eye of the artist could see.

"Come in, Inspector." The invitation was friendly and warm.

Reg noted the display of some of Hendry's work placed around the immaculate living room.

Admiring the work served to initiate the conversation.

The skill of the artist was to be seen in the wide variety of subjects. Wild birds, animals and human figures.

The Inspector took his time in going round the exhibits, remarking on their merits as he saw them.

Hendry was pleased to see the Inspector and acknowledged the praise with a certain degree of modesty.

"How long ago is it since you lost your wife, Hendry?"

The man was slightly startled. It was obvious to an intelligent man that the Police were not altogether interested in his art work. Why, then, this matter regarding his young bride?

"It was May last year. The twenty-first to be exact. That is the last day I saw her."

The man's expression changed visibly. "Why do you ask, Inspector?"

"Certain evidence has come to light which requires your co-operation."

Reg pulled the envelope from his pocket.

Hendry watched intently. Expectantly. The movement of the Inspector's hand seemed to mesmerise the man. He looked on as two rings appeared in the Inspector's hand.

"Do you recognise these rings, Hendry?"

The man's hand shook as he reached forward and took the rings. He held them close to his face and began to read inscriptions on the inside. The effect was tragic. Hendry dropped his arms by his side and attempted to hide his feelings by turning his head away from his visitor. There were no tears. The man had shed all his reserve of tears.

Reg was patient and sympathetic. He waited until Hendry had regained some composure.

"They were my Susan's," Hendry gasped. "The rings belonged to my wife. Where did you find them?"

"Hendry, we have to come to know each other quite well over these last few days, and I am asking you now to try to hold yourself together when I tell you were we found the rings. In the estate, you must be aware that there is a family crypt and it contains the tombs of past generations of the Harper-Nelson family. It was by mere coincidence that Campbell, the reporter, noticed that the entrance to the crypt had been disturbed. He went into the crypt and began to nose around. He is a pretty thorough chap and he found the skeleton in one of the tombs and spotted the rings."

It is difficult to describe Hendry's reaction to this grim explanation. His remorse could be seen in the change in his weather-beaten complexion. He looked pale and had sagged into his chair completely shattered.

He was reliving the experience when all his hopes for the future with his young, attractive Susan were suddenly brought to an end.

"I'm really very sorry to have to be the one to tell you all this about your wife, Hendry, but you will understand how it is absolutely necessary that we have all the facts brought into line."

"In the crypt. In the estate? My Susan."

Hendry shook his head and then gradually his attitude began to change, remorse and signs of the effects of what he had been told overcome by as anger welled in his heart.

He spoke slowly. Every word deliberately chosen, revealing the determination building within the man like a vulcano gathering its power to erupt.

"I can think of only one man who would have the opportunity to murder my wife, Inspector, and that is the Laird. The bastard. If I have chance, he will suffer for every day I have spent in this house. Our house. We made it so that we could enjoy the life we thought we had ahead of us. My God, but that bastard will pay for this."

In this mood, Hendry was an extremely dangerous man. He would be difficult to control.

In fact, the man's reaction had gone far in excess of what Reg had anticipated. He was alarmed at the growing ferocity of Hendry's attitude as retribution was clearly displayed in his manner.

"There is something else you can help us with Hendry. Can you tell me if your wife ever had an injury to her right wrist?"

Hendry paused in his secret rage and looked at the Inspector.

"Susan broke her right wrist when she was a schoolgirl, why do you ask? Did you. Was there? I mean to say, did you find a broken wrist on the remains in the crypt?"

"Yes, Hendry, the skeleton in the tomb was wearing these rings and the right wrist had been broken."

"So, it is my Susan, she has been in the bloody place all this time."

Hendry lapsed once again into his grief.

"Hendry, we have taken you wife's remains and placed them in a suitable coffin. However, when the time comes, you can do whatever you wish to see that she has a respectable burial."

"You've been very kind, Inspector and I appreciate what an ordeal it has been for you to tell me about this. I am very grateful."

"You understand that there are certain formalities to be completed but they won't delay matters for long."

Reg had had many a rough passage in his life in the force but he found himself glad that this ordeal was over.

Hendry sat for a while after Reg had left his home. It had taken him a year to come to terms with the loss of his young bride. He looked around the room, the furniture they had both enjoyed choosing for the home they had hoped to build. The wedding photograph in its gilt frame. Photographs can be startling reminders of the past.

He recalled the frantic search which had followed the disappearance. The pain and the suffering. The uncertainty. The many questions. Where? Who? Why? How? The tragedy. The loss of all he had ever dreamed about.

Someone, somewhere must know what had happened on that day about a year ago when she had smiled and waved her hand and threw him a kiss as she set out for the fateful walk in the country.

He passed his mind over all the contacts he had made with the residents of the village and he was satisfied that he had no grounds for suspecting any one of the locals and it was then that he realised that the only person he had not talked to was the Laird. The man of mystery, who seemed to be as illusive as the "Scarlet Pimpernel'.

The man who lived in the mansion, surrounded by its shroud of trees and guarded by the equally, incomprehensible McKenzie and his double-barrelled shotgun.

The man who seemed to appear from nowhere to halt the progress of anyone seeking to visit the big house; turning them back from whence they came in no uncertain manner.

Hendry dressed himself and set out for the manor. He was determined that he must talk to the Laird. He must satisfy himself regarding the impressions he had acquired from the remarks of the people in the village. He was in no doubt that Inspector knew about his association with Mira; He admired the man's discretion. The Inspector had avoided any reference to Hendry's present private affairs.

Now all his past had been brought into light, Hendry resolved to protect Mira's feelings. She must be assured that the love they had been sealed with a kiss.

This dramatic twist could not possibly spare him the agony of reviving old memories; the pain and the agony of not knowing; yet, it served to lay his questing mind at rest. His wife was no longer "missing'. She was dead. Both he and Mira had survived the scathing rebukes liberally handed out by the minister. Now they could look to the future in the knowledge that they were both free to live their lives together without the fetters of the past.

It was a fine day with a light, warm breeze. Hendry decided to enter the estate through the lodge gates. This would take him past the crypt which he now knew was used to conceal the bodies of his wife and the young girl.

It was important to him that he should see the tomb. To see the temporary burial place of the woman he loved.

He mulled over the present position. The victim suffered and is no longer suffering. The survivor lives a lingering nightmare of pain and despair.

To his surprise, his progress was not interrupted by the gamekeeper who must have had more pressing matters to attend to elsewhere.

The entrance to the crypt was tramped by the Police when they removed the bodies from the tomb. The door was not locked and he had a feeling of unease as he entered the resting place of the family Harper-Nelson.

There before him was the stone container. The lid had not been replaced on top.

The man stood for a while. Looking and sensing the awful interior, with its dressing of cobwebs and dust.

There was no glass in the slotted windows, allowing weird beams of light to spread inwards in all directions and the wind to create an unearthly symphony for the dead in their tombs.

Regular rows of tombs were placed in tiers of three around the walls. Each bore a brass place, naming the deceased.

Hendry was not in a mood to observe the common decencies required to be shown in such places. He had no idea what he was looking for. He simply went ahead, removing the dust from the nameplates on the tombs and reading the inscriptions.

Then he noticed the dates. The dates on the plates were of considerable importance. 1908, 1900, 1905.

1905? The date was twenty-five years ago. Who had been buried in 1905?

Hurriedly, he wiped away the thick layer of dust and read "Ronald Harper-Nelson."

It was now apparent that a man bearing the family name had died over twenty-five years ago, and had been buried in the tomb.

He then turned his attention to where his wife had been placed and, being a practical man, carefully inspected the stonework. He found himself asking how one man could have moved such a heavy stone slab and this led to the possibility that some kind of lever or tool had been used.

In the gloom where the shafts of light could not reach he found the answer to his question. Lying, buried in dust, a metal crowbar. Hendry knew enough about evidence to avoid touching the metal bar and now his attention was concentrated on the stonework of the tomb.

There was the tell-tale mark of the tool used to lever the lid open, and he realised that this could be a vital clue, if fingerprints were found, identifying the person who had handled the metal.

He left the crypt and made for the bleak, derelict home of the enigmatic Laird. Surely, he mused, there must be something wrong with someone who would allow such deterioration to what must have been a magnificent mansion, and, surely, there must be something wrong with a man who dispensed with all his servants with the exception of the housekeeper and the gamekeeper. Where he was known not to socialise and had no friends around him. Living as he was reputed, in isolation and mystery.

The green Talbot with its white walled tyres was standing nearby; a sure sign that the owner was at home.

Martha appeared in answer to his knock.

"Yes?"

The lady in black could have been mistaken for a pillar of stone.

"I wish to speak to the Laird."

"Who are you?"

"My name is Hendry Ashford and I live nearby."

"Wait." There was no attempt at courtesy. No sign of friendliness.

Hendry stood on the doorstep much longer than was necessary. The lady in black reappeared.

"Come." She led the way indoors and passed through a door which obviously led to her own domain.

As he waited, Hendry found himself contemplating the moment when he would face the man of whom he knew so little. The man with the power inherited from his forebears.

Social status had little effect on Hendry. He had no feelings of humility and didn't share the general reserve shown by most of the local residents.

Hendry watched the man as he descended the pink marble stairway. Erect, arrogantly, showing no sign of how he felt, and bearing that air so commonly attributed to the few who own the wealth and have the power and authority that money provides.

It was difficult to see what lay behind the mask. The expressionless countenance. There was no smile. No indication of any intention to be cordial or otherwise.

"My housekeeper tells me that you wish to speak to me?"

The voice was cultured and well modulated, but had little effect on the visitor. Hendry was not intimidated and found himself calmly taking the measure of the man standing before him.

He hadn't the advantage of an expensive process of training in cultural and eloquence given to the few. He took his time. He had nothing to lose and, unknown to him, the arrogant Laird was sensing a feeling of unease. Who was this man? Police? Newspapers? He certainly was not behaving in the manner generally accepted as customary by the locals.

"Your housekeeper is quite right, I do wish to speak to you, that is if you can spare the time. If not, perhaps it may be possible to make an appointment to see you."

"What is it you want to speak to me about?"

"Then I take it, you can spare me the time?"

A question and no answer? Who is this man? The relationship between master and servant had once again been disturbed.

The cunning mind of the man was already preparing the way to retreat from this strange and seemingly dangerous encounter with someone of whom he knew so little.

"I would like to take you back in time to about a year ago."

"Yes/"

"It was about a year ago that a young married woman set out from the village to enjoy a stroll in the country air. She was never seen again."

The Laird was clearly off his guard. Reference to the disappearance of the young woman was unexpected.

"The young lady who went missing was my wife."

"You have my sympathy, of course, but I cannot see how you think that I can help you. After all, it is a year, is it not, since your wife was last seen?"

Hendry had a feeling that the moment had arrived. What he was about to say would obviously be extremely significant to anyone who might have any knowledge of the event in question.

He noted that the Laird had acquired a certain degree of confidence during their brief encounter. His composure was about to receive a shock. What he was about to say would undoubtedly unnerve the rather too confident Lord of the Manor.

"My wife has been seen since and quite recently too."

The colour drained from the mask and knowing this, the Laird suddenly began to pace about the hall,

119

hoping to conceal the reference to the sighting of the missing person and its effect on his attitude.

Hendry knew. He knew that this man was responsible for his wife's death. Everything about the man. His strained, cautious manner and, come to think about it, the man had not asked where the lady had been seen and in what circumstances. Was she alive? Was she dead?

Why had he omitted to ask the obvious questions? Was it not plain to see that the man had knowledge of what had occurred on that fateful day about a year ago?

Hendry was not a man of violence. He had difficulty in stemming the growing anger and concealing his rage. He knew that he was now dealing with matters which could tip the balance of innocence and guilt.

On the other hand, the Laird was striving to control the turmoil in his confused mind and to unscramble the alarm which caused his heart to race completely throwing him off balance.

It was suddenly time to rid himself of this threat to his freedom. This stranger with the ability to cause him such distress.

"Tea? Ah, yes. We must have tea."

Martha answered the bell obediently. She stood silently; waiting upon her master and his command.

"Tea, Martha."

The lady in black withdrew as silently as she had arrived in the hall. The two men waited in silence, each unwittingly exposing the tension which now occupied their thoughts.

Martha soon returned with the silver tray and left.

Why this sudden change in the Laird's attitude? To a stranger? Was it something he had said, which had caused the unexpected lapse in his confident manner. Had what he said touched a nerve?

The tea was most unexpected. The Laird offered his guest a cup and placed sugar and cream at his disposal.

It occurred to Hendry that the sight of his wife in a photograph might disturb the man and he produced the photo from an inside pocket. It also occurred to Hendry that the Laird's fingerprints might prove to be useful.

The Laird took the photo and looked at it. He was observed closely. The man's hands shook visibly.

"So, this is your wife?"

At this stage, the rules of the "game' were reversed. It was now the Laird's turn to move a pawn. He dropped the card near to Hendry so that his guest would pick it up.

As Hendry stooped the drug was added to the tea.

Hendry placed the photo in his pocket and somehow sensed that all was not as it should be.

The Laird was doing his best to seem disinterested in the process of stirring tea.

A sudden decision to offer the tea was significant and suspicious, to say the lease. There was obviously a need for caution here. Hendry knew that he had somehow to avoid drinking the tea.

He wasn't as innocent as others who had been invited to partake of a cup of tea in the big house, and as he reached over, he allowed his tie to enter the cup, saturating it with the tea. There was no alternative. He had to be bold about this situation.

"Oh, I', so sorry. That was clumsy. I've ruined your tea and my tie."

He rose and made the announcement he knew would produce the result planned. He had also a sample of the contents of the cup.

"By the way, the body of my wife was found in your family crypt, and she wasn't alone. There was another body in the tomb."

"Why, that cannot be. No-one has been in the crypt for years."

Hendry knew that the man was now off his guard. He was satisfied that he had obtained the evidence of the man's involvement in the disappearance of his wife and decided to end their conversation whilst he had the initiative.

He left the house and decided that his next move would be to discuss all that had transpired with the Inspector.

CHAPTER TWELVE

Hazel Murray lay on a wooden floor. Dazed, and recovering from a sleeping potion, she could barely make out her surroundings. As her eyes regained their focus, she became aware that she was in a large room and that there was light coming from a tall window.

As her faculties returned, she struggled to her feet and walked towards a door.

It led to a bathroom. She felt very thirsty and went to the sink. The water was sour. It had lain in the piping for a long time but she had to drink. It did not occur to her to allow the water to run for some time. She might have been excused for this oversight, considering her condition.

Her mind was clearing but she found that she could not understand where she was. How she had come to be there and why was she in this large, empty room? She had been drinking tea.

Then she saw the bed. A very large bed and the chains. What on earth were they there for? Chains attached to the four corners of a bed?

Although she was a virgin, she had little doubt about their significance. She felt a sudden sensation of fear.

The sound of a key in the lock attracted her attention. Martha appeared, her white waxen expression and her silence as she laid a tray on the floor, only served to increase the feeling of alarm.

Martha withdrew and closed the door, before the teenager had time to think about what she should do.

She was hungry. She ate the bread and drank the tea, and it occurred to her that this meal could also contain some sinister ingredients. Too late now, she had eaten most of the bread and sipped most of the tea.

Fortunately, there seemed to be no adverse effects from the contents of the tray.

She felt slightly better and walked rather unsteadily to the window. The tall opening was covered with spider's webs. She could barely see the surroundings outside the house, but nevertheless, she was sure that she had seen a man standing facing the house taking a photograph.

The man turned and left.

Banging on the door with her fists didn't last for any length of time. Flesh and bone can only take so much punishment. She noticed a wooden chair. That would do, and yet, persistent hammering with a chair on the door produced no response.

So, she was a prisoner. The cold expression on the silent woman in black gave her no reason to hope that she would come to the girl's assistance.

The noise created by the chair served only to emphasise the hollow sound and echo of the empty house.

Fear began to possess the girl and through the fog of growing panic, her mind began to exaggerate the future and what might happen to her. Why had she been imprisoned? Why had she been drugged? How long had she been in that room? She felt so helpless.

The questions came flooding into her mind.

She tried to control her fear with reason but panic overcame her efforts to be calm and the panic led to terror as the reality of her predicament presented itself.

She was exhausted and must have fallen asleep, because, when she opened her eyes she noted that darkness had fallen.

The key scraping in the lock and the door hinges complaining about the lack of oil and Martha had returned.

"Come" she said. "You must leave this house at once."

She led the frightened girl down the pink marble stairway and opened the panel in the front door.

"Go, girl. Go and don't turn back."

The woman closed the door and Hazel found herself in the fresh air wondering which way she should go. Alone.

She recalled that she had been driven through a driveway to the house and made for the opening in the trees where she could see in the half light of a summer evening.

Adrenaline activated her muscles and, before long, she was pacing her way towards the lodge gates.

The light of a car appeared ahead and brought her to an abrupt stop. She suddenly remembered the car with its white, walled tyres and her reaction was spontaneous. She dived into the cover of the shrubbery.

Had she been spotted by the driver? Was the driver the man with the brown, leather boots? Without waiting to find out, Hazel crashed her way through the undergrowth without any sense of direction.

She stopped to listen. Someone was following her. There was no sign ahead of her to let her know which way to turn. She went blindly on in her panic-stricken flight from the unknown, treading the shrubs in her wake.

Her instinct urged her to move but reason intervened. She began to realise that whoever was following her could pass on if she silently moved off the track.

This idea seemed to be one way to avoid an encounter with the pursuer.

She crawled into the shrubs and tried to conceal herself as well as she could.

She lay in silence. That is, as silently as her breathing would allow.

She had been wise to stop her mad stampede, and to lay low because soon after she had concealed herself, she heard the heavy breathing of the large man pass her, crashing onwards; obviously intent on capturing her.

Hazel lay in the shrubs for some time, listening in the dark. Listening. Her ears tuned to the slightest whisper. The breaking of a twig. The movement of some nocturnal animal brushing against leaves.

The would be assailant moved on, getting ever distant from her until there was silence.

She heard the car start and move off and through the trees, lights could be seen moving in the direction of the big house.

The girl had never been in the vicinity of the village of Craigmire. Surrounded by the shrubs and the trees, she might as well have been on the moon. She had no sense of direction and no knowledge of the district of where she might find safety.

She must have rested for about half an hour, when she heard the roar of the car being driven at speed and its lights flashing past, onwards towards the lodge.

Then the silence again, as the noise of the car faded into the gloom.

Feeling slightly confident that the threat to her safety had gone up the drive with the car, she began to make her way towards to drive, knowing that at least she would reach the main road.

"Dinna be feared, lassie."

Hazel screamed. The voice in the darkness came without warning.

"Ye're a' richt noo, dinna be scared I'll nae harm ye."

It was the gamekeeper. McKenzie stood in front of her with his shotgun.

"Noo, I want ye ti trust me and ti follow me." The man began to walk towards the lodge gates.

With a great deal of uncertainty, the girl followed some yards behind. She was afraid to speak, and as they drew nearer to the lodge gates, she began to feel more assured.

McKenzie had some idea about what the young girl must be thinking and talked to her as they walked and when they reached the lodge, he pointed in the direction of the village and told Hazel that she would find help there.

It was a well-kept secret that he and Martha had been having an affair for many years. Martha's sphinx-like mask hid the kind of soft spot which happened to sympathise with the rugged nature of the man with the gun.

Indeed, unknown to the residents of the village, McKenzie spent more time in Martha's quarters than he spent in the lodge, where it was assumed that he lived his solitary life.

He had a feeling that all was not well at the house. That young girl obviously was greatly disturbed and in fear, confirmed his suspicions that the Laird was not all he seemed to be.

The front door of the house was open. This was unusual. The Laird insisted on that door being kept closed. It was always to the servants entrance that the gamekeeper crept, under the cover of darkness but this seemed to be an exception. He went into the house through the front door, disregarding the standing order of his employer.

The door to Martha's quarters was open. This, again, was unusual. Martha never left that door open.

McKenzie began to feel uneasy. He walked with caution. There was something wrong.

Was Martha in the kitchen?

Yes, Martha was in her kitchen, dying!

She was sitting; leaning forwards on to the top of the wooden table. A large knife had been driven through her body, pinning her to the wood.

McKenzie rushed to her side. He leaned closer and heard the woman whisper, "the Laird, he...", and then she was dead.

Blinding rage surged through the man. There was no doubt in his mind that it had taken a strong hand to drive that knife into the body and to lodge it into the wood.

What could be the reason for this murder? Had that girl anything to do with it? She was distressed and in terror! The Laird was also in a hurry when he left the estate some time before.

McKenzie was saddened at the loss of his companion, but his violent nature was also something to be taken into consideration.

He had worked for many years with the owner of the Craigmire estate and had managed all the affairs. He gathered the rents and paid the bills but in all that time, he had still to hear a word of appreciation from him.

He knew that he was now obligated to report what he had found to the Police, and, leaving everything intact, he left the house and made his way to the village.

Donald's mother was well known in the area. Many of the local residents owed their life as she plied her skills as the "Mrs McKay and her wee black bag.'

During these post-war days of economic depression, a health service was only a "twinkle in the eyes' of the politicians, who could have earned their salaries by laying down the rules of play for what eventually became the National Health Service and which has, by reason of greed and intrigue, been eroded into a mere shadow of what was originally intended.

Service existed solely to those who paid a weekly contribution into an insurance scheme. The so-called friendly societies who provided the all important stamped card which was demanded as proof of membership.

The black bag was cramped with instruments, potions and all the accessories required to serve as First Aid to the needy.

The kindly lady would never accept reward for her services. She carried out her chosen mission silently and efficiently, in the full knowledge of the limitations as a lay person, and never hesitated to call the services of a doctor when she considered such a measure to be necessary.

It was natural that she would be called to attend to the young girl in the control and when she entered the room, she went immediately to her and began to gently explore her condition.

Satisfied, she took command.

She was persuasive and her attitude left no doubt that it would be foolish for anyone to ignore her orders.

"We must gi' that lass some privacy. She seems to be suffering from shock. Now, have ye sent for the doctor?"

She scanned the faces for an answer and shook her head in exasperation. "Dearie me, you men, I suggest that you call the doctor right away."

The control room was buzzing with activity with Inspector Gilmour arrived.

Mrs McKay was standing by, directing operations. She had improvised a clothes line, which supported blankets, forming a screen around the girl.

Reg took in the scene at a glance and nodded appreciatively to Mrs McKay.

Then he turned to Donald and Monica and they both knew that they were obliged to offer the Inspector an explanation.

"We have no idea who the girl is. We were out for a walk along the main road when she ran into us. She was in an awful state and nearly collapsed when she collided with us."

Monica added, "She appeared to be dazed, she wasn't looking where she was going, just running and staggering blindly along the road."

Reg moved over to look at Hazel and turned to Mrs McKay.

"Is she going to be all right?"

"Oh I think so. Her breathing is regular and her pulse rate is just a wee bit high, but otherwise I think the lass will recover quite soon. We have sent for a doctor."

"Splendid, Mrs McKay, you have been a great help."

He was aware that the case was out of the ability of one man to handle, and was relieved when Headquarters in Dunfermline advised him that reinforcements were on their way.

If she was asked to be honest, Mrs McKay would grudgingly admit that she and the minister's wife occasionally failed to see "eye to eye'.

There seemed to be a certain element of rivalry between the two ladies.

Mrs Davidson just happened to visit the control room at that moment and, as was her custom, assumed an air of command.

Mary McKay was having none of this; she was busy washing her hands at that moment and nodded to the lady of the manse. She saw immediately the opportunity to involve the minister's wife in a "Christian act', and said, "I've just had a wonderful idea now that you have appeared, Mrs Davidson. Could you find a bed in the manse for this poor girl?"

Mrs Davidson was "checkmate'. There was no way out and to crown all, the suggestion had not been her contribution to the problem.

"Why, certainly, of course, the poor girl must be looked after and I can think of no better place. Mrs McKay, you think of everything." It is possible that the minister's wife really meant what she said on that occasion.

It was convenient that a stretcher was kept in the village hall and the men soon had everything set to carry Hazel to the manse.

Inspector Gilmour revealed that he had more faith in Mary McKay than Mrs Davidson, to ensure the girl's safe-keeping and asked Mary to go to the manse "Just to see that all was well."

The local residents didn't miss a trick. They were out-of-doors, watching the procession in silence as Hazel was conveyed to the manse.

Who was she? Where were they taking her?

I was important that, whatever Hazel had to say would be recorded and Mrs McKay was asked if she would let them known about any change in her condition.

Life in the village had seen a complete upheaval in the otherwise tranquil day-to-day existence and lifestyle of the residents.

The men loitering at the well, hopeless, with no specific interest had suddenly something new to talk and argue about.

The general store was seldom empty. The bell about the door rang continuously as customer entered, not so much as to make a purchase, but to gather another grain of excitement raised by the present tragedy.

"Nellie Dean', the favourite song, had been replaced by low pitched murmuring and occasional rowdy exchanges. Speculation was high on the subject of murder as Joe Penman drained another barrel of their favourite brew.

Without exception, no-one who knew the rugged, weather-beaten gamekeeps, would have expected to see the man in his present state.

McKenzie entered the village, dejected, his head hung low and clearly very distressed.

The gossips at the well nudged and nodded each other as they watched the man who had, for so many years, held himself aloof from them, reduced to a pathetic image of the former insufferable minion to the Laird. A man who would not tolerate arrears in rent and would evict entire families regardless of the weather or their state of health. The man who seldom spoke, except to say what was absolutely necessary in order to carry out the duty of factor, gamekeeper and general aid to the owner of all the land around the village. The Craigmire estate.

McKenzie staggered towards the village hall and disappeared from view into the Police control.

He sat on a chair and held his head in his hands.

Inspector Gilmour stood quietly for a while watching the man. What next? Everything seemed to be happening in this village of terror. What had shattered the hard man and brought him to his knees?

"Mr McKenzie, how can we help you?"

Grief and pent-up emotion was suddenly realised in the man sitting in the chair. "Martha's dead!" he said, in a quiet, subdued tone.

"Martha, the housekeeper at the manor?"

"Aye, Martha, my God, what a sight! She was pinned to the kitchen table wi' a big knife."

"Take your time, Mr McKenzie, take you time and tell us what you have seen."

McKenzie drew himself together and lifted his head. Reg could see that the man was deeply affected by what he had seen.

"I met the lassie on the drive and took her to the main road, then I walked doon ti' the hoose. Ye see, I kent something wiz wrong because the Laird had driven oot and away at a fair speed. When I reached the hoose, the first thing I noticed wiz the front door. It wiz open."

"Is it unusual for the door to be left open?"

"Aye, it's never ti be left open, but it wiz. It wiz open and when I went in, I saw that Martha's door wiz open. Noo, Martha always kept her door closed. That's the door to her quarters and the kitchen. When I went in ti the kitchen, I saw her. There she wiz, sittin' at her table. She wiz bent forwards and the knife had gone right through her body. There was blood a' o'er the place."

The man subsided into silence and held his head in his hands.

"You must have had a shock, Mr McKenzie, now you can go home and rest for a while. We can talk to you later."

"Aye, I need time ti' think and I kent that I had ti' tell ye."

With that McKenzie rose and left the control. He made his way to the main road and to the lodge where he lived, no doubt, turning over in his mind the future when it would not be possible to share his sorrows with the lady in black at the manor house.

CHAPTER THIRTEEN

Most of what the gamekeeper had said had been written down by D.C. Penman, who had listened intently to every word.

A full, official statement would be required at a later date but the Police had now another point on which to focus their attention.

The summer sun had gone and the day was almost spent, but the Inspector knew that the urgency was apparent. He could not delay action, not only on McKenzie's garbled statement but on what Campbell had reported about the crypt.

As soon as the reinforcements arrived, the Inspector called them together and began to outline the chain of events and how he suggested that they would proceed to deal with the investigation.

Detective Sergeant Spence and two uniformed men were appointed to examine the crypt, whilst Inspector and D.C. Penman would visit the manor, where Martha was reported to have been murdered.

Before they set out on their respective tasks, the doctor poked his head around the door and told them that he had examined the girl at the manse, and had left some medicine with Mrs McKay. "The lass's all right. She is suffering from severe shock. McKay knows what to do."

With these brief words of reassurance, the man was gone. He was always in a hurry to get somewhere.

Mother Nature must have been smiling with pleasure at the freedom with which she had been allowed to envelope the residence of the family Harper-Nelson in a shroud of ivy and moss and, as if by way of a slight apology for her intrusion, adorned her handiwork with masses of blooms. Wild flowers and colours, only She can use.

Within the walls, Inspector Gilmour and D.C. Penman surveyed the stiffening corpse of the once proud lade in black.

Martha had indeed been murdered. There was no doubt. Here, once again, the full resources of the local Police force would be required to act, another investigation initiated.

D.C. Penman was left to stand by the scene of the murder, whilst the Inspector travelled to the crypt.

There he met D.S. Spence and two uniformed men, busily engaged in threading their way through the mass of evidence associated with the remains of the skeleton in the tomb and the body of the young girl.

A constable was ordered to relieve D.C. Penman and his colleague was sent to the village to call in the murder squad.

Reg noted that what Campbell had told him had been accurate. Whoever had placed the girl's body in the tomb had neglected to replace the heavy stone lid.

Otherwise, the existence of the murdered girl might have remained a mystery.

Uniformed Police took over the duty of standing guard at the murder scenes, whilst the detectives returned to control.

There was a great deal to discuss about a series of incidents, and they agreed that measures were required to be stepped up in order that whoever was responsible for the deaths would be stopped and dealt with according to the law.

Their fortunes seemed to take a turn for the better when the team working on the Blyth case arrived with the brute, handcuffed and in his usual sullen mood.

Everything had gone to plan as expected. Blyth had taken the ladder and entered the bedroom, where the body beneath the sheets was obviously intended to be his target. The man had brandished a knife indicating his intention to threaten his proposed victim whilst he carried out his beastly act of rape. Within seconds, he had been subdued, handcuffed and a charge was made against him.

The Andersons would sleep better and with great relief now that the man had been arrested.

The villagers were treated to a new source of excitement as the convoy of Police vehicles passed through the village on its way to Dunfermline and the news of the arrest was made known to them.

The church yard marked the last resting place of former generations with its headstones and monuments and vases of flowers. Yet, unknown to their residents of the village of Craigmire, the graveyard was the secret resting places of former victims of violence and sexual pervertion. The bodies of innocent young women cunningly deposited beneath the site of burials which occurred from time to time.

John Greig had dug the graves for many years. He cut the turf and shaped the digging to perfection with his shiny spade.

It was odd that no one had any suspicion regarding the friendly assistance the old man had from Blyth. The fact that Blyth would render assistance to anyone without payment was entirely out of character where he was concerned and known for his greed and indifference to the circumstances of others.

It was indeed a fact that Blyth was known to assist the grave digger on frequent occasions. Taking the shiny spade and allowing the old man to rest a while. It was, of course, all part of a cleverly disguised method of burying the bodies of victims murdered by the Laird.

It was so easy. All Blyth was required to do was to hide the body until a grave was required to be opened. He would then watch and made his move at the stage when the grave was almost completely excavated. He would appear at the right time to offer a "helping hand'.

Then, by digging an extra layer at the base of the grave, he was in a position to move the body under cover of darkness and to cover it with earth.

On the day following these clandestine operations, the bereaved would assemble around the opening in the ground and the "dearly departed' would be ceremoniously lowered gently to rest on top of the unknown victim below.

Now that the Inspector had Blyth in custody, he was able to recollect all that had transpired in his dealings with the man.

He consulted the carefully recorded statements made by Blyth and by Campbell and it was now clear that the recorded reference to digging required more attention.

He talked the matter over with D.C. Penman and both men agreed that they were prepared to face the villain in the interview room.

When the three men were settled in the room used to interrogate those who had come into contact with the process of Law and Order, they had before them a man who was obviously capable of perpetrating the most sordid kinds of criminal activities. They had acquired sufficient evidence of the man's limited mentality to cause them to be confident of an early route towards a confession of guilt and of participation in crimes committed in the area and presently under investigation.

Blyth found his surroundings in the Police station at Dunfermline familiar ground.

He had been held there on many previous occasions and was no stranger to the officers who moved silently around on their various duties.

He was a sorry sight, seated, alone, obviously experiencing the mental torture of anticipating the "uncertainty' of what would happen to him next.

The Inspector led the way to the interview room and took a seat behind a desk. Blyth sat facing the Inspector and D.C. Penman stood behind the prisoner which served as means to distract and, on odd occasions, to prevent violence getting out of hand.

Reg took his time; toying with the papers in front of him. Another delaying tactic designed to further cause stress and tension and to prolong the devasting effect of anticipating the "uncertainty'.

He looked up and smiled at the man seated before him.

"Mr Blyth, you are in trouble now, arn't you? You have been a silly boy."

Blyth made no comment.

The Inspector continued. "Now we want to talk to you about another matter and it is a bit more serious than the charge you are now facing. Tell us about your grave digging."

The sudden switch and the threat brought about by this clever deviation had the desired effect.

The man was speechless.

"Mr Blyth, what about your grave digging?"

The Inspector was taking full advantage of his initiative. Blyth appeared to have resigned himself to what had become obvious to him. He could see no way of escaping the consequence of his foolish mistakes.

"I didna' kill the lassies."

"You had something to do with their deaths, Mr Blyth"

"I only buried them"

"Can you tell us who killed the girls?"

"The bloody Laird. The man's mad. He took the lassies to the Big Hoose and when he was finished wi' them he cam' for me"

"What were you asked to do?"

"The Laird planned the whole thing, he had the idea ti get the bodies into the graves and I had ti dig the bottom oot so that the bodies widna' be seen."

The man seemed to be unaffected by the atrocious nature of the crimes he had played such a gruesome part in.

There was now sufficient material to fulfil the legal requirements in the writing of a statement and the Inspector proceeded to pen the amazing details of what had been discussed in that room.

A confession which read like some horror story; describing the last moments in the lives of young, innocent girls as they experienced fear and terror and the ravishes and lust of the perverted owner of the lands at Craigmire.

It was possible to take Blyth's low intellect into consideration when reviewing the history of the crimes committed.

The man had really to be pitted. He had developed bone and muscle in his large six foot frame but somehow, his mind had remained in a simple state. During the early stages of his life he had been taught to steal and to swear and use his physique to address the unbalance of normal social relationships. His simple mind was incapable of sympathy and feelings and Reg managed to calm the anger within him when he reflected on the brutality he was recording. It was hard to visualise the criminal carrying a lifeless body of a young girl and placing it in an unseemly grave.

When the statement had been written it was completed when Blyth signed it and in the process, revealing the fact that he used a pen with great difficulty. The Inspector informed Blyth that it would be necessary for him to visit the cemetery and to point out the graves used to conceal the bodies and ordered him to be returned to his cell.

Meanwhile there was another resident who had a score to settle.

McKenzie was a violent, ruthless man and his employer was well aware that he had not only the Police to worry about. He had McKenzie. The gamekeeper was a man to be reckoned with.

As far as McKenzie was concerned the hunt was on. The man of the woods knew all the Laird's habits and many of the places where he would be likely to be found.

Lizzie Duncan's Store was more than usually popular. There was so much going on. The locals were affected by the growing excitement caused by recent developments in the serial murder investigations. Blyth''s arrest and the movements of the Police officers as they carried out their inevitable tasks. The villagers were anxious not to miss the latest episode in this the greatest diversion from the hum drum life in a rural community.

Wee Harry Downie had gleefully accomplished another successful day "off school' and whistled his way through the assembled crowd rattling two pennies in his trouser pocket.

He pushed his way through the characters standing eagerly and expectantly under the canopy of hardware suspended over their heads.

The clamour was so loud that the boy had to shout.

"Lizzie"

Lizzie was, at that moment, deeply engrossed on conversation with other customers as they discussed the arrest of the notorious Mr Blyth.

"Harry Downie, whit's yer hurry? Whit di ye want?"

"I'm waitin' for my toffee."

"Here ye are" Lizzie scooped the penny from the counter and turned to face her friends.

Harry peeled the paper from "Highland Cream Toffee' and crunched a segment contentedly.

"The Police are a' at the cemetery"

How strange the effect of what a small boy could have on a crowd of women. Harry; young as he was; actually enjoyed this moment in the limelight.

"The Police in the cemetery, Harry, did ye happen ti' see whit they were doin'?"

"Auld Grieg the gravedigger is up there and the Polis are diggin a grave."

"My goodness, dinna tell me that they are diggin' a grave"

Moments later, Lizzie found her store deserted. Her friends had vanished and were hastily making their way in search of more sensations.

Wee Harry stood at the door contentedly munching his toffee innocently unaware of the effect his announcement had on the departing crowd.

Armed with all the necessary authorisation, Inspector Gilmour was directing the excavation of a grave pointed out by Blyth as one he used to conceal the burial of one of the murder victims.

A slight hollow in the grass over the grave gave every indication that the coffin had caved in and was no longer supporting the earth above it.

This also gave the experienced officers a good idea of the condition they could expect the corpse to be in.

Uniformed officers gently persuaded the gathering sight seekers to keep their distance from the scene of operations; must to their annoyance. After all; this kind of thing didn't happen every day.

It was late afternoon when the black Police van left with its grisly cargo followed by several Police cars. Blyth could be seen seated between two sturdy uniformed officers.

Another two graves would be opened to reveal the remains of victims of the terrible murders which surprisingly had been committed under the noses of the villagers without their knowledge.

Dental records and lists of missing persons were all that the Police would have to rely upon to identify the contents of the graves and to establish, beyond doubt the guilt of the man who had perpetrated the horrific crimes.

CHAPTER FOURTEEN

Hazel's aunt and uncle had travelled from St. Andrews and were relieved to find their niece at the manse, although her condition gave them cause for concern.

Mary McKay was able to assure them that Hazel would be fully recovered once she had come to realise that there was no longer any need to fear.

When she opened her eyes, Mary McKay was there to smile and attend to her needs. Hazel was naturally aware that her surroundings were strange and Mary explained how she happened to be in the manse.

Mrs Davidson was also present to lend her support and the appearance of the minister in his "uniform' reassured her.

The doctor knew his job and the medicine had worked wonders on the patient's morale.

She was able to sit up and chat to her friends and, at times, refer to her nightmare experience in the house of death.

The arrival of her aunt and uncle completed her recovery and Mary McKay relaxed. She knew that she had performed yet another successful "First Aid'.

With the tension and the terror receding, Hazel began to find her way back to a semblance of normality.

The events of the past few days persisted on flooding her thoughts reminding her of the terrible threat to her life.

She kept seeing the waxen image of the lady in black and heard the hollow voice, "Go, girl; Go."

She relived the aimless race through the shrubs and it was only then that she became aware of the physical effects she had sustained. The lacerations and abrasions caused by the undergrowth and shrubbery. The bandages placed with loving care by the kindly lady and her wee black bag.

In the company of her aunt and uncle she knew that she was safe and secure, but the vivid reality of what she had been subjected to continued to invade her composure.

It had been recommended that she should seek medical advice when she reached St. Andrews and her aunt was well aware that her niece would need careful counselling for some time to come.

The Police were extremely thoughtful and had used their sophisticated lines of communication to contact Hazel's parents and to inform them that their daughter was safe.

Needless to say, Hazel's parents were in the midst of celebrations with their daughter as soon as they could travel to St. Andrews.

Gradually, she was able to recount the horror of her experience and what she had to say was of crucial importance in the case of the Laird of Craigmire.

The events at Craigmire had far reaching effects in many areas involving skills of experts in pathological investigation, observations and application of regulations and the law.

The Craigmire murders had been widely published under such headings as "The Craigmire Murders', or "Serial Killer at Large', as well as other superlative concoctions deliberately intended to exploit the sensational developments in the village of fear.

Publicity was not given to the work and dedication of those who were responsible for the accumulation of evidence and facts which would ensure the conviction of the person or persons who had perpetrated the crimes.

The men and women, it may be argued, who, behind the scenes, preferred anominity. The uniformed and plain clothes Police scientists, lawyers and advisers.

The machinery of law and order maintained to preserve the freedom of the individual to live a normal life.

The mass of evidence produced so far, did not convict any individual, despite the circumstantial conditions surrounding the incidents and the undoubted presence of suspects during the estimated times of death in each of the cases under examination.

Priority lay in the production of proof beyond any doubt.

At this stage, it was considered essential that the landowner should be located and questioned about his movements during the past months. So far, the elusive Laird had eluded the watchful eye of the law.

Margaret Wilson found dead and lying in a ditch, whilst her personal belonging were found in a cellar at the manor house!

Marks on her body, matching in every detail, the chains found in the bedroom in the big house!

The body in the tomb identified as Janet Farley, and her personal belongings found in the cellar at the house. Her body, bearing marks of chains which matched the chains in the room upstairs!

The skeleton in the tomb wearing rings, positively identified as having been worn by Susan Ashford, the wife of Hendry Ashford!

Collectively, each victim could not yield proof beyond doubt to convict any person.

The law required evidence which would established the guilt of the murderer, where representations for defence could not produce an acceptable brief in opposition to the Crown procedure and prosecution.

There remained only one case undisputed to prove that the Laird had broken the law.

Hazel Murray was alive. She could bear witness to abduction and unlawful imprisonment and she could identify the Laird as the man who had wilfully deceived and imprisoned her.

Hazel's personal belonging were found in the cellar at the big house, and the one mistake made by the murderer was found in the fingerprints on her handbag.

The prints belonged to the Laird.

Police had searched the big house and found the room with the chains and other evidence, which revealed the sadistic nature of the murderer.

They had found fingerprints on the large knife which had caused the death of Martha Heslop. The fingerprints belonged to the Laird.

Inspector Gilmour and his colleagues ran through the list of items related to the case. The reports. The statements. The evidence, such as the personal belongings of the victims. The chains, together with other less important items, which would stand to convict one man for the killings.

The big house was now the centre of intensive Police activity.

The evidence of the atrocities which had been committed was being methodically stored in the Police van parked in front of the house. The drugged wine. The chains found in the bedroom and in the cellar; an "Alladin's cave'.

With seemingly careless abandon the criminal had placed the personal belongings of his victims in a cellar.

Margaret Wilson's clothes; Hazel Murray's luggage and her No.2 Brownie.

Ironically, when the girl had taken a photograph of a peacock she had inadvertently snapped the Laird standing in the background; establishing his presence in the Glen and providing a positive link with the discovery of the body in the tomb.

The knife used to kill the housekeeper provided fingerprints known to belong to the Laird, another important piece of evidence linking the man with a crime.

The mass of evidence providing an ever increasing case for indictment of one particular individual was all that was required to bring a man to answer the accusations in a court of law but the Inspector was only too well aware of how well-oiled palms in high places could find sufficient grounds in defence of a client to oppose whatever might be considered to be the irrefutable fact of guilt.

His sole aim was the search for proof, and something Hendry had said began to occupy his thoughts.

It was about that brass plate he had seen on the stone tomb.

Had this been fully considered?

This was a job for the boys behind the desks. There was a growing feeling in his mind that the Inspector was not dealing with the true heir to the estate.

He recalled that the brass plate had borne the inscription Ronald Harper-Nelson and this could have been a brother; an elder brother and therefore the heir.

What had happened to cause the death of the elder brother?

Who would know? Could there have been some sinister conspiracy leading to the death of the man in the crypt?

Hendry called in at the control and was fortunate to find the Inspector on duty. His detailed description of his encounter with the Laird was of great interest. Reg had not spoken to the man and it is important in any circumstances to know the character of the person under scrutiny.

Hendry's characterisation was most helpful and the forensic laboratory would certainly be able to isolate the type of drug which saturated Hendry's tie.

The team searching the big house were concentrating on the quarters occupied by the housekeeper.

D.S. Spence, leading the search, had a feeling that the lady in black could not be entirely innocent, or unaware of what had taken place in the house, and if so, what kind of person could allow the scene of terror to continue for so long, when young women were subjected to the sadistic practices of a man who was obviously mentally disturbed?

Was it fear of some threat to her own safety? Was it loyalty to the family she had served for half a century? Watching the Laird grow from childhood to the monster he had become?

Martha's bundle of keys implicated the woman in as much as that they provided access to any part of the house, including the chains found in the bedroom upstairs.

The marble clock about the fireplace was obviously expensive. Ornamented with jewels and gold. D.S. Spence reckoned that such a valuable piece was out of place in the servant's quarters and deserved more attention.

He checked the time with his rather large, but inferior, pocket watch. He moved closer to examine the fine workmanship and the detail which gave the clock its distinctive quality.

The gold pendulum swayed silently behind a glass frontage and an ivory block forming part of the base with its gold inlay completed the overall design.

Sharp eyes spotted the defect. The block of marble was slightly out of position. A gentle touch with a forefinger revealed a secret drawer.

Martha's diary had been found. A detailed record of what had taken place in the house over a number of years. The writing was neat and explicit and the words condemned her employer beyond any doubt. Dates and times, as well as comments on the Laird's ever-changing moods. His anger, his charm and even an explanation for the presence of the clock. Martha wrote how she had been given the previous timepiece for "services rendered'.

She described how she buried her head in the pillows to overcome the screams of torment and terror coming from the room upstairs.

The detective's hands trembled as he read the testimony of the dead woman's thoughts turning the reality of the document he held in his hands.

A complete record of the crimes which had been committed in the house of horror.

This was a written testimony and irrefutable proof of the guilt of the Laird.

The folded document was a certificate of birth. There in his hands the Inspector had proof of the existence of the true heir to the Craigmire estate. The birth certificate of the son of Ronald Harper-Nelson and Martha Heslop, Chambermaid.

It became immediately obvious that this boy would be the rightful heir but where was he now? Was he alive?

Reg fumbled with the diary and eagerly searched the pages for any reference to the boy which might provide a clue regarding his whereabouts, and there it was.

The boy had been fostered by a couple known to Martha in 1920. Tearfully, the then chambermaid, described how she had to part with her new-born son and hand him over to Robert and Helen Dickson, on the insistence of the Harper-Nelson family.

Martha had conveniently entered the occupation of her friend, Robert Dickson as a "Railwayman'.

Reg turned the matter over in his mind. This document placed a great deal of emphasis on the circumstances associated with the death of James, the elder brother of the man who claimed to be the Laird of Craigmire estate. How had he died?

The secrecy was understandable. After all, the gentry would not admit any misbehaviour or promiscuity. No shame, no guilt would be attached to a member of the family elite.

The Dicksons had readily agreed to the terms laid down by the family. The boy was to be named Dickson and the secret of his origin was not be revealed.

The writing went on the describe the love affair which had developed between the son of the Laird and herself and how it had been so difficult to maintain the secret when she made frequent visits to her friends, the Dicksons.

Finally, she described how James, the father of he child had died due to tuberculosis and how she had to accept the younger brother as her employer.

CHAPTER FIFTEEN

The green Talbot saloon parked at the Lower Railway Station was kept closely under observation. The Police were well aware that the parked car could mean two possibilities. The owner had travelled south or north.

The weight of evidence against the man justified the measures taken to apprehend him if he was foolish or desperate enough to use the car.

The search for the killer had reached national proportions and the public were asked to assist by reporting any sightings of the "Man wanted for questioning'.

James Harper-Nelson was desperate. His attention to the news was creating panic. The net was closing and he knew it.

Uppermost in the minds of the hunted is the desire to disappear. The predator had become the prey. He was conscious of his appearance in the expensive tweed suit and brown leather boots.

He was also aware that it would be dangerous to discard the clothing. This would certainly lead the Police to the point where he had been. It would be a marker.

It seemed, logical, therefore that he should change his appearance and destroy the clothes he was wearing.

Such was the calculating mentality of the criminal.

He would allow his beard to grow and his hair to appear unattended. He could wear a cloth cap and an old raincoat then, out of the blue, he found the answer to his dilemma.

During the 1930s, the Territorial Army was a popular means of escaping the starvation of civilian communities. In the T.A., one would be clothed and fed and bedded down in a certain degree of comfort. He was aware of just such a camp used by the Army, located north of the town.

Under the cover of darkness he made his way north and settled at a point where he would watch the activities of the camp.

He was experiencing all the rigours of the hunted. Hunger and lack of sleep as well as the chill of the night air.

As dawn broke, he could see the tents and the soldiers going about their duties. A tent nearest to the boundary fence seemed to be a likely target and as it happened, the army unit was preparing for some manoeuvres and a march out of camp.

There would be only a small number of men left and this would be a good opportunity to enter and obtain anything which could be worn other than the clothes he was wearing.

Many an ex-serviceman will have no difficulty recalling the scene in the billet where, in compliance with "Regulations', the soldier's kit was laid out in a strict pattern. Blankets folded and placed, ready for "Inspector'.

The precision created a problem for the fugitive. An item missing from the tidy display would be noticed immediately. However, the Laird smiled at the thought, it would be the soldier who would be punished for the loss of whatever he managed to take from the tent.

It so happened that he was able to dress himself with a uniform, which complied reasonably with the standard required.

No-one saw the pseudo territorial slip through the boundary fence and disappear into the woods.

It isn't difficult to imagine the aggravation in that billet when the weary soldiers returned.

Dressed as a soldier made the Laird conspicuous, but it served as a disguise. He bundled the clothes he had been wearing and moved off towards the village of Craigmire.

His last hope was to seek the assistance of his gamekeeper. As he lay concealed, waiting until it was dark enough to approach the lodge without being seen, he hoped that the man would be at home.

McKenzie opened the door when he heard the knock. He had had time to think over the past events. He had reached the conclusion that he would deal with the man if ever he was given the opportunity.

This is perhaps why he gave the Laird the impression that he could expect some friendly assistance. The gamekeeper could even manage a smile.

"Can I come in, McKenzie?"

"Why, surely, just step inside. You might be seen and you certainly don't want that to happen, do you?"

The fugitive was completely exhausted and thankful for the chance to relax.

"I need you help, McKenzie, and I know that I'm asking a great deal in asking for your assistance."

"And whit might that be?"

"I believe that I can arrange to leave the country, but I will need some time and you will have to meet someone for me. You understand that I can't be seen running around like this." He indicated the uniform.

"Jist where di ye think ye kin get a boat aboot here?"

"Burntisland. There is sure to be a ship there at the aluminium works and I know some of the people down there."

"How are ye goin' ti manage ti travel ti Burntisland?"

"I'll need to move during the night, especially in this rig", displaying the uniform.

"Ye are bound to be hungry and there's some bread and jam on the table there. Noo, help yersel' and have a wee lie doon and I'll gan oot and see if I kin find a bike for ye. Change yer clothes."

The hunted man was only too eager to ease and rest for a while and eagerly accepted the gamekeeper's suggestion.

McKenzie closed the lodge door gently and made off into the dark. He had other plans to attend to and they were not quite what the employer expected.

He made for the heap of manure in the corner of the field which by now had reached considerable proportions and he carried a garden fork.

When he reached the midden, he began to dig a deep trench in the manure. His intentions were obvious.

He was dealing with a man who had shown no compassion when he had rudely ended the lives of so many young women and apart from the criminal acts, he was not known to have committed, there was the reputation the arrogant aristocrat had earned by his manner and abrupt intolerance of any obstacle in his way.

The Laird had fallen into a deep sleep, but stirred slightly alarmed when McKenzie returned to the lodge.

"I've managed to find ye a bike and I think it would be best for ye to get goin' noo."

The Laird had eaten a sandwich and the rest had revived him slightly. He had no hesitation in following his employee out into the dark of night to the corner of the field where the manure was stored.

There was no suspicion in his mind as he followed McKenzie over to the manure.

The gamekeeper did not hesitate. He raised the shotgun and the Laird's inglorious existence ended in two loud blasts from the double-barrelled gun.

It didn't take long to cover the body with manure and to leave no trace of what had taken place on the midden.

People hearing shots in the night were not unduly alarmed. It was quite a familiar sound to them as they knew that the man with the gun was forever on the prowl.

The "Slow Cooker' had begun its work and, given time, there would be little to identify a man reduced to a jelly-like mass.

McKenzie had nothing to lose. He, after all, had tuberculosis and knew that he had not long to live. He had also considered the events leading up to the final act of judgement on the man who had wilfully committed the crimes. It might well have been right to comply with the law and allow the courts to pass judgement on the accused, but deep in his mind there lingered the dread that the man with all the resources of wealth at his disposal, would escape the penalty he deserved.

The slow cooker was already generating the heat which would carry out that penalty without cost to the crown and the state. There would be no lawyer's fees and court expenses. No newspaper headlines and, as far as he was concerned, the feudal lord would soon be a jelly-like mass.

Hendry Ashford felt deprived of the revenge burning in his heart. He stood with the residents of Craigmire, watching the flames reach high in the sky over the woods which, for so long, had shrouded the manor.

The family residence of the Harper-Nelsons, with its priceless treasures and all its secrets and whispering walls, lit the sky for miles around. The house of horror was reduced to a smouldering ruin.

Inspector Gilmour had his suspicions but didn't take any action to follow a "hunch'.

Before he disposed of the body, the gamekeeper remembered the belt worn around the waist. It was in that belt the Laird kept his money and, knowing the man, it was certain that he had charged his belt with sufficient reserves to meet the expense of his flight to freedom.

Some time had passed when the relatives of the victims received mysterious envelopes each containing £2000.

There was no explanation.

The rugged, giant of a man had no need for money. He grinned as he locked the flaps and sealed the "wee gift' to those he knew could never be compensated for the loss they had experienced at the hands of the man in the house of horrors.

As time went by the trial grew colder and the file on the Police records lay on its shelf amongst others marked "unsolved'.

Old Sandy Thompson finally laid his hammer to rest and, having no relatives, left the business to Donald McKay.

Donald couldn't get used to the absence of the old man at his forge. The man with the bald head and carbuncle.

Later, there was great excitement in the village as the young lovers married.

For some time, it took the residents some considerable effort to find something new to talk about. The bells could still he heard. The bawdy songs still rang out from the "Plough' on Saturday nights and throughout the day the children's voices could be heard parroting the times tables. "One and one are two; two and two are four', and about all the young voices, if you cared to stand and listen, you might have heard one particular voice just a shade lower in pitch than the others.

The voice belonged to a little boy called David McKay, the son and apple of Monica's eye.

If ever you should pass through the village of Craigmire about midnight, and you find yourself in the vicinity of the place where they store the manure.....don't linger too long!

POSTSCRIPT

A little boy sat on the gatepost at the bottom of the garden, where he lived, alongside the railway marshalling yard situated halfway between the town and Craigmire.

He overlooked a seemingly limitless expanse of gleaming, steel rails, twisting and turning in a maze which served to align trains into their proper order for destinations all over the country.

The air was heavy with the unmistakable smells of superheated steam, oil and smoke from the engines, shunting, puffing and pulling their loads of freight wagons in response to signals given by the shunters, who coupled and uncoupled the rolling stock - separating them according to their particular assignment.

Gordon Dickson had learnt most of the sequence of events as the unending stream of goods wagons moved through the yard.

The signals, which when operated, would indicate the departure of yet another long line of goods wagons to distant parts.

Loads of coal and farm machinery and livestock trumpeting their complaints to the world outside their crude, open transports.

He had learned to recognise the coded signals coming from a nearby signal cabin.

"Train on line', one would say. "Line clear'.

There was an important message with every sound of the bells and indicators.

The boy wondered at the complexity of all that he saw. There was so much he couldn't understand. There was so much he wanted to understand. He wanted answers to the why's and how's and the when's. Intelligent, he would often make his own interpretation of the scene of the moment. Imagining all kinds of wonderful situations involving trains and steam engines, which today, when steam is part of our history, would be the envy of many a small boy.

There was little else for a small boy to do, isolated as he was, from the surrounding towns and villages where all manner of things occurred to fire the imagination and widen the experience of life.

The "Yellow Brick Road', to that other world was nothing more than a railside track which he and his family trecked in all weathers when need arose to "go to town'.

The moment he was waiting for was bout to arrive.

He heard the bells in the signal cabin ring out loud and clear "Train on lice', they said - "Train on line'.

The code heralded the most important event of the day. The Aberdeen to London express was always on time. From far into the distance, he could hear the shrieking steam whistle scream its warning to whatever lay ahead.

In an instant, it thundered into view. An avalanche of fire and steel and sparks. Alive, vibrating, wheels gleaming and invisible drive rods beating an unmistakable rhythm in time to the click of the rail joints.

Flashing past at a steady sixty to seventy miles per hour, the passengers silhouetted against a dim interior, glimpsed for a fleeting moment and then they were gone. Anonymous. Each with a personal reason for being there, men, women and children. Hundreds of them, moving at speed over the rail track no doubt blissfully unaware of the turbulence and friction created by flanged wheels in contact with steel.

The power and the drama excited the boy seated at the garden gate. There was so much to see and to listen to in these fleeting moments. Then, it was gone. In its wake, a vortex of smoke, hot oil and steam passing out of sight.

Those with vested interests in roadways and motorised transport undoubtedly reaped a large harvest from the rusting rail tracks.

When we consider the senseless equation of comparative costs between road and rail traffic, and the effect on the environment, we begin to see the financial gain there is to be realised from taxation alone.

The thunder of the express was in contrast with the comparative quiet of the puffing of the little engines marshalling the trains into line.

During the halcyon days of "steam', there was no rusting rail tracks. Rusting through lack of use. Throughout the entire country, the railway lines reflected the prosperity which had escaped the notice of greedy investors.

Where is the logic behind the "derailment' of major routes in the country in preference to the millions of motor vehicles despoiling the air we breathe.

Gordon descended from his perch on the gate post and made his way to the cottage.

He looked surprised to see two strange men with his stepmother, and she was prepared for his reaction. She knew that he was a shy boy and would be happy to make a quick retreat from the ordeal of facing strangers.

"Gordon, come and meet Inspector Gilmour and Mr Walker."

Gordon reluctantly stopped in his tracks and turned to face the two men.

Reg recognised the boy's predicament and smiled reassuringly. We have brought your mum some good news Gordon. Don't you want to hear what we have to say?"

Mrs Dickson placed her arm around the lad and edged him forwards. "This is Mr Walker and Mr Gilmour," she said.

Gordon hesitated but extended his hand to both men in turn.

Mrs Dickson asked her visitors to be seated and Gordon stood by her side.

Mr Walker treated the matter gently. He knew that the boy would not be able to understand the significance of what he had to say about inheritance and birthrights. That could wait. All that was required at that particular moment was to establish the existence of the heir to the estate at Craigmire.

The men accepted the offer of tea. The Dickson home was immaculate and the smell of furniture polish and clean fresh linen made the home-baked scones more acceptable.

Soon after the preliminary meeting the Dicksons were called to the office of the lawyers, Walker and Stubbs, and from that point onwards, the true identity of Gordon Dickson was known.

The legal matters relating to the estate were brought into line and it was agreed that the estate should be continued in Trust until the young heir was old enough to take charge of his own affairs.

Fortunately, the boy had attended school in Dunfermline and was not known to the villagers of Craigmire. They, in turn, had mysteriously been advised that the new heir to the estate had been found and it was only natural that much speculation would be exercised on who he might be and where he would be found.

Arrangements were made to educate the lad and to provide for his needs whilst his foster parents would continue to care for him as their own.

There was not much to see at the site of the "big hoose'. The fire had been thorough. However, in one particular area where Martha's quarters had been located, the fireplace had survived the inferno and on the mantleshelf, a marble clock inlaid with gold remained.

The Police had managed to protect the remains of the house from would-be looters and it gave Reg Gilmour a strange feeling of pleasure to hand over the clock to the young heir of Craigmire.

Perhaps in time to come he would learn of the woman who had owned the clock with the golden pendulum, and who she really was.